# Corn on the Cobb

# Corn on the Cobb

## AN EAST DEVON COSY MYSTERY

## P.A. NASH

*My grateful thanks for Tom Miller from Exeter in allowing me to use his photo of the Cobb at Lyme Regis.*

# Dedication

To the whole Nash family - from Elsie's Bow to Resource Angel. Love, as usual, from PA.

**Pop backstage into the world of 60's chart star Cornelius Spooner for a mixture of music, murder and cosy mystery. Meet Cornelius, his band, the Portobello Crooners and his six wives.**

During a quiet weekend away at a Country House Hotel near Lyme Regis, Frank and Ella Raleigh find themselves caught up in their deadliest case yet.

Accidents? Murders? Suspects with alibis, motives and opportunities – it's all there.

A gentle cosy read in the tradition of Midsomer and the two Agathas. Renew old acquaintances in an evolving whodunit set around the glorious East Devon edge of Lyme Regis.

Treasure the walks. Uncover the clues. Solve the mystery.

Book Four in the East Devon Cosy Mystery series.

# TABLE OF CONTENTS

# CHAPTER 1

# A HARD RAIN'S GONNA FALL

The heavy rain fell out of the grey sky exploding rather than splashing on the slippery paving stones. The ancient, crumpled suitcase was heavy and getting heavier by the minute. The bus stop was still too far away. If it wasn't for the adrenalin and the anger, then now would be the time to just give up. To lie down in the dripping hedge and let all the woes and injustices of the world just take their sorry toll.

Despite the circumstances, plans were still buzzing around.

A quick, firm push with both hands. An over balance and then gone. Don't wait around for the splash or the scream. Leave the scene of the crime as soon as possible. You don't want to get caught red-handed. Revenge.

A smile appeared on the dripping face.

"Cornelius Spooner, one day I am going to make you pay."

# CHAPTER 2

# HEARTBREAK HOTEL

Frank and Ella Raleigh were about to wave goodbye to the village of Otterbury. The car was cleaned and prepared. Frank had once again checked the windows and doors in their house were all firmly locked. Ella made sure the two suitcases were stowed away in the boot and on the back seat of their car before settling down in the passenger seat and awaiting her husband.

"All ready?" asked Ella as he clambered into the driver's seat.

"Yes, I don't think we've forgotten anything."

"We're only going away for the weekend. You'd have thought we were emigrating to Australia."

"Can't be too careful. I know this is gentle East Devon, but things seem to happen to us down here."

"Well, this weekend is going to be different."

"Yes, happy anniversary."

"And to you too. Now, can we get going?"

"Don't worry. It won't take us long. It's not as though we're even leaving the county. Through Sidmouth and

Colyford and we'll be there."

Their destination was the Cobb Country House Hotel on this side of Lyme Regis. Since Ella had won the Ottery Lottery, life had been hectic and their wedding anniversary was the perfect excuse to get away for a few days, away from the responsibility of overseeing Kennaway Coopers.

"Now I'm not complaining," griped Ella, "but it will be lovely not to wake up and have to think about Kennaways. Not that I'm saying that George and company can't run the place…"

"They've done a darn good job so far," laughed Frank, "with or without our help."

"True."

Frank drove sedately through sleepy Sidford and up the steepness of Trow Hill.

"On your left is Harcombe Valley."

"Yes, every time we drive this way you say…"

"What do I say?" Frank knew he was being teased.

"That Harcombe Valley is your favourite valley, the epitome of an East Devonian valley."

"Well, it's true."

There was a moment of silence as they reached the top of the hill.

"Perhaps one day we'll move there."

"You'll need to rob a bank first!" beamed Ella.

"I think not!"

"Or maybe join the Board of Directors at the Donkey Sanctuary. I think they own most of the land around here!"

"Yes, they might have a rundown cottage going spare."

"There's nothing rundown about Donkey Sanctuary land.

Everything's in spit-spot condition. Only the best for our beloved donkeys."

"There, there, Ella," frowned Frank. "They do a lot of good work for the community."

"Yes, I know, but sometimes I wish some of our less well-off humans were shown the same level of kindness."

By now, they had passed the turn-off to Beer. The traffic was light as usual and Frank could enjoy pootling along, past the Seaton Tower and then down Harepath Hill.

"Look at that view," cooed Ella, "All across the Axe Valley. It's glorious."

They meandered into another quiet sleepy roadside village. Colyford.

"Did you know that Colyford elects a mayor?" asked Frank.

"But it's only a tiny village - not a town or city."

"It's an ancient borough and stretches back to 1230."

"So, they've had a mayor for almost 900 years?"

"Not quite. The mayorship died out by the late 1800s according to their website."

"Oh, you've been searching the internet again for those wonderful facts of yours?"

"Guilty as charged."

"Well, tell me more about Colyford. I can see the Tramway. I know all about that."

They were stopped at the level crossing gates as one of the Seaton Trams glided across the road.

"Not only does Colyford have a mayor. They also elect a Constable, Mace Bearer and Flag Captain each November at their meeting of the Borough Burgesses."

"Burgesses or burgers?"

Frank laughed as the level crossing gates opened and

they moved off again.

"Do they have a barbecue?"

"Ella, this is in danger of descending into the realms of fantasy!"

"You've been watching Dad's Army again."

They crossed over the winding River Axe and made their way up another hill towards Lyme Regis. A while before the road dipped down into Lyme Regis, Ella called out "Here it is!"

Frank eased the car left into the grounds of the Cobb Country House Hotel.

"There we are," said Frank, "Half an hour door to door."

"It may be half an hour but it's like entering another world," wowed Ella.

Cobb Country House Hotel stood like a luxurious version of an Agatha Christie villa in some 1930s village. Red bricks framed the large sash windows of the ground floor, terracotta Devon tiles covered the upper floor between tudored wooden gables. The roof was lined with brown slates sloping in intriguing angles. Was that a turret at the corner of the west wing?

"It's like a grander version of Kennaway House," remarked Ella.

Frank parked on the sandy coloured gravel alongside several other cars, all much cleaner and more expensive than his.

They both got out and rather shyly made their way to the front entrance. The door opened as they approached it and a gentleman dressed in what appeared to be a butler's uniform stood aside and welcomed them into the hotel.

"Good afternoon, madam. Good afternoon, sir. Welcome to the Cobb Country House Hotel. My name's Reeves. If you would be so kind as to register yourselves at our reception desk."

"Thank you," blustered Ella.

"May I have *your* names, please?"

"Yes, it's Mr. and Mrs. Raleigh."

Reeves imperceptibly nodded his head.

"Sir, if I may take your car keys, I will endeavour to make sure your vehicle is parked safely and will then transport your luggage to your room. How many suitcases."

"Two. One in the boot and one on the back seat."

"Thank you kindly. Your keys?"

Frank gave him the keys as if hypnotised.

The attractive young blond-haired girl at reception signed them in. "Did you have a pleasant journey down here?"

"Yes," said Ella. "It wasn't too long."

"I can see you're from Otterbury from your registration. I love the Otter Valley."

"Yes, so do we," replied Ella.

"Is that your book?" asked Frank pointing to a book on the counter.

"No," she said. "I expect one of the staff left it here. *The Royal Art of Poisoning*. A bit too gruesome for me. There, that's your registration complete. Please follow me and I'll show you to your room."

They climbed the main stairs and along a short corridor before the receptionist stopped in front of one of the bedroom doors.

"Here we are. You're in the Peek Room. It's named after the family who developed the estate around here in the eighteenth century."

The room was elegantly decorated in grey with a king-size bed and views out across the road towards the sea.

"The rooms are opened and locked by using this smart card. Please try not to lose it. We do have spares but…Well, there's a coffee machine and free wi-fi. The hand-crafted bed was designed and made in fashionable London and has Egyptian cotton linen and goose down pillows. If there's anything you need to know, please contact either myself at reception or speak to Reeves, our hotel butler. I do hope you enjoy your stay."

Having reached the end of her immaculately presented script, the girl handed the keys to Frank, curtsied and left the room.

Ella bounced down on the bed. "This is lovely. Hand crafted in fashionable London! What a treat!"

Frank looked out of the window. It was so quiet, even quieter than Otterbury. Look, you can just see Lyme Regis."

Ella had found the information folder and was leaving through it.

"There's an outdoor heated swimming pool, a maze, archery, gardens and even an old medieval well."

Frank turned away from the window. "Let's go exploring then!"

After three attempts with their smart card, they swiped their door closed and made their way out through the front entrance and around the side of the house. They soon discovered the swimming pool and behind it, they noted the maze. It wasn't on the scale of Hampton Court or Escot, both of which they had circumnavigated with some degree of success in the past. However, there was a look out post. They climbed the steps and waved at a lady of similar age to them making her way out of the maze towards its entrance.

"Good afternoon," Ella shouted.

"Hello," the lady replied.

"Well done, you've beaten it!"

The lady had emerged from the maze and smiled at them before sedately making her way to the front entrance of the hotel.

Frank and Ella ambled around the outer hedge of the maze before wandering through the gardens. They discovered the medieval well. Its stone edging was crumbling and covered with moss. The well itself was covered by a circular wooden slab.

"I wonder if they bought that cover from Kennaway Coopers?" said Frank.

"That doesn't look too safe," murmured Ella. They strolled along gravel pathways through the well-managed gardens filled with an abundance of plants and bushes. The colour and aromas were almost intoxicating. Ella discovered a swing seat sheltering beneath a tall evergreen hedge and they spent an agreeable half an hour gently rocking in the shade of the late afternoon sun.

Ella and Frank drifted around the gardens passing the archery gallery before arriving back at the far side of the hotel. They went through the front door and made themselves comfortable in the guest lounge. Magazines and newspapers were stacked neatly on the smart coffee table.

Frank leafed through the local paper, the *Bridport and Lyme Regis News*. He mused over the upcoming *Guitars on the Beach* festival. He was just about to point it out to Ella when the lady from the maze walked in with a book and sat down by the sash window. She nodded to Ella, "I hope you enjoyed the gardens."

"Yes, they're lovely."

Frank was still engrossed with the paper when he spotted a familiar name in the What's On section.

"Amelia Nutwell!"

"Pardon," said Ella.

"Amelia Nutwell. She's in the local paper. She's the president of the Cornelius Spooner Fan Club."

"There's a name from the past!"

The lady from the maze looked up. The gentleman who welcomed them to the hotel - the butler - stood at the door of the guest lounge.

"And..."

"He's performing tonight. Down in Lyme Regis. Amelia's drumming up business. Listen. 'Do come down to the Cobb this weekend and hear one of Britain's truly great singers. Cornelius will be singing all his hits from the Sixties along with his backing band, the Portobello Crooners.'"

"Gosh, I remember him when I was young. Is he still alive?"

"Must be because he's on stage tonight in Lyme Regis. They've called the whole evening *Corn on the Cobb* ."

"Amelia goes on to say that it's a free outdoor concert put on by the *Guitars on the Beach* team to say thank-you to the people of Lyme Regis for supporting the *Guitars on the Beach* festival."

"Let's go, it could be fun."

There was a momentary silence.

The hotel butler was still standing by the lounge door. "Would sir and madam require an early evening meal? So that you can attend the er, musical performances?"

"Er, yes, please, er…."

"Just call me Reeves."

"Er, yes please, Reeves, that would be lovely."

"And madam," Reeves began turning smoothly towards the lady from the maze.

"No, thank you. I have no intention of seeing that old has-been ever again."

Reeves tapped his fingers rhythmically on the door panel, imperceptibly bowed and left the room.

"Is he really a has-been?" asked Ella.

"An old, tuneless, ugly has-been and a skinflint like no other. And I should know."

"Why?" asked an intrigued Frank.

"I married him."

# CHAPTER 3

## WOODSTOCK?

After a very acceptable early evening meal at the Cobb Country House Hotel, Ella and Frank drove the short distance across the Dorset border into Lyme Regis. It took some time to find a parking space and even more time to find their way down Broad Street and along Marine Parade to the Cobb.

There were large groups of people on the sands facing the dark stone harbour wall of the Cobb. A compact covered stage had been erected on the walkway next to a long low building. The evening light was fading, and the stage lights were beginning to bite through the surrounding area. A group of musicians were on stage playing some Sixties sounding music. When they finished the song, there was polite, semi enthusiastic applause mixed with sporadic cheering. The four musicians waved at the crowd and strode off-stage.

"Have we missed him?" asked Ella.

The Master of Ceremonies, the compere came on-stage.

"Thank you, our very own - BeeSharps!"

A couple of people nearer the stage screamed their approval. Looking around, Frank and Ella could see groups sitting on beach chairs in the sand with elegant picnics. Some youngsters were swigging bottles of what looked like cider. Other youngsters were filming snippets of the evening on their smart phones.

The MC continued. "Next up - another local group. In fact, a duo from here in deepest Dorset. Ladies, Gentlemen, boys and girls, give a great big Jurassic welcome to Shelby's Elbows!"

A guitarist and a bassist almost ran onto the stage and bowed to the crowd. The guitarist in the requisite dark glasses shouted out, "Hi, I'm Martin, he's Phil and we're Shelby's Elbows."

"And this," interjected Phil, the bassist, "is *Yesterday's Voice!*"

"Quite appropriate, really," remarked Martin, before crashing out some fast rhythmic strumming.

For the next thirty minutes, the crowd was thoroughly entertained by a variety of songs - some covers, a few Beatles songs, some original, all of them fully enjoyed by the growing crowd. The crowd, now fired up, forgot about their food and drinks and cheered.

"These two are really rather good," enthused Ella.

All too soon their set was over. The crowd roared their approval and called for an encore.

The MC sauntered on stage shaking his head. "I'm sorry, ladies and gentlemen, no encore tonight. Got to keep to schedule! You can see Shelby's Elbow most weekends somewhere in the Dorset area. Go onto their website, find a gig and go and cheer them on. One more time for - Shelby's Elbow!"

There was another raucous cry of delight from the crowd

as Frank and Ella looked around. The beach and promenade appeared to be packed with families, couples, beer drinkers and youngsters. Everyone was smiling, chatting and giving the impression of thoroughly enjoying their evening out.

Ella's eyes glimpsed two familiar faces.

"Look, there's the butler from the hotel, Reeves, and he's with the lady from the guest lounge."

"You mean the one who said she was Cornelius' wife?"

"Yes."

"Where?"

"They were over there by the steps." Ella looked again. She shrugged her shoulders. "Oh, they've gone now."

"Perhaps she's off backstage."

"Yes, if she's his wife, then she'll be getting the VIP treatment."

"I thought she said he was a has been and she had no intention of ever seeing him again?" Ella mused.

"Must have been persuaded to change her mind."

There was another resounding roar as the MC re-appeared on stage. He raised his hands to quieten the crowd. "Now, ladies and gentlemen, boys and girls, mods and rockers, fans of British rock and roll. May I introduce to you, the star of stage, screen and vinyl, the man with the voice of granite and the heart of gold - Mister Cornelius Spooner and his Portobello Crooners. It's Corn on the Cobb!!"

There were a few screams from those gathered nearer the stage and scattered applause from the rest of the densely packed crowd. A few groups of older looking rockers raised their cider glasses in the air and hollered out some unintelligible words of advice as the Portobello Crooners - a drummer, a pianist and a double bass player walked briskly on stage. They were all clothed in matching sparkling blue suits and immediately started playing a fast rock and roll shuffle. After about thirty seconds, from stage left, appeared Cornelius. He had a bright sparkling golden suit and had an electric guitar swung around his back. He turned to the crowd, waved with both hands and shouted "Hello, Lyme Regis. Hello, dinosaur country. Here's one dinosaur who's not ready to be a fossil-just yet!"

A few people near by Frank and Ella laughed.

Cornelius strode to the very edge of the stage and pointed to the screamers in the front row. "Are you ready to rock and roll?"

The screamers screamed.

The cider drinkers replied "Yeah!"

A couple of the older ones around Frank and Ella nodded sagely.

"Then let me take on a sea cruise!"

The band picked up the rhythm and crashed out an acceptable version of Huey "Piano" Smith's *Sea Cruise*.

*So be my guest, you got nothin' to lose*

*Won't ya let me take you on a sea cruise?*

As the sun dipped below the horizon, Cornelius Spooner created a party atmosphere on the Cobb. All the songs, as far as Frank could tell, had a seaside theme to them. He recognised *Surfin' USA* and then a sped-up *Sitting on the Dock of the Bay*.

*I'm just sitting on the dock of the bay*

*Wasting time …*

A slower almost gentle version of *Under the Boardwalk* was followed by Terry Dactyl's *Seaside Shuffle* - without the accordion. Cornelius and his guitar made a creditable attempt at *Wipe Out* and then had the whole beach, and especially the cider drinkers, joining in the next song's chorus:

*We all live in a yellow submarine ...*

A rip-roaring rock and roll medley followed to the delight of young and old and after nearly an hour of active music, the crowd were dancing, drinking and singing along.

"Let's bring it down a bit," mumbled Cornelius, "I'm not as young as I thought I was!"

The band moved into some slower numbers *"Sailing"*, *"The Water is Wide"* and *"Harbour Lights"*.

*I saw the harbour lights*
*They only told me we were parting*
*The same old harbour lights that once brought you to me ...*

Frank felt he was showing his age as he recognised himself singing along silently.

Ella held on to his arm and commented. "He's a good guitarist. I love his solos. Short, loud and exciting."

Frank nodded before smiling at her. "Yes, every solo gets greeted with a cheer."

"Well, he's good."

"And he knows it."

"You mean the way he bows every time?" Ella smiled. "He does rather milk it!"

"Strange then that his guitar isn't plugged in."

Ella stared closely, "You're right! Do you think he's playing one of those wireless guitars? Like they have wireless microphones?"

"No, look, off-stage."

To the left of the stage, partly hidden from view, stood a youngster, dressed in shirt and jeans holding a guitar. People were moving in front of him but both Frank and

Ella could see his guitar was plugged into an amplifier.

"Watch out for the next guitar solo."

Sure enough during the middle of a rather laboured version of the Beatles "*Octopus' Garden*"

*We would shout and swim about*

*The coral that lies beneath the waves*

*Oh what joy for every girl and boy*

*Knowing they're happy and they're safe*

Cornelius played a solo. He strutted around the stage. Now and again, he posed in a statuesque Rock God position. At the end of the solo, he turned to the audience, bowed and then carried on singing.

"That wasn't him. That boy off-stage played it," Frank commented.

"And he was very good! Why doesn't he give him some credit?"

"Perhaps he will at the end of the show."

The slower songs continued, and the crowd began to get a bit restless.

Someone near the cider drinkers bawled out "Rock and R-o-l-l!!" It was so loud that there was a moment's silence.

"Thank you, Lyme Regis, you've been a wonderful crowd." Cornelius stopped to gain his breath. Someone from the wings threw a towel to him. He wiped his forehead and wrapped the towel around his shoulders.

"It's getting late, and we all need our beauty sleep. Boy, it's hot up here." He wiped his brow with the towel once more.

"I'd like to finish off the evening with our biggest hit. "*The Night is Still Young*" You may remember it. So, it's a big thank you from the Portobello Crooners and a big thank you from me. The Night is Still Young!

The band moved into a typical early sixties dance rhythm and Cornelius with his hand on his heart crooned the words as he had done so many times before.

*The night is still young*

*And so are we*

After another melodic guitar break and a bow from Cornelius, he started moving towards the side of the stage. He turned once more to the crowd, waved and then clutched inside his jacket at his heart. He staggered, dropped his guitar neatly into the hands of the pianist and stumbled to the floor.

"My word, is he OK?" cried Ella. There was a gasp from the crowd. The band carried on playing, apparently not quite sure what else to do.

Cornelius lay there for about fifteen seconds. It seemed like a lifetime. He then pushed himself up on his arms to a sitting position. He turned to the pianist and asked him something. The pianist passed the guitar to a be-suited man who had come towards Cornelius before moving across the stage and picking up Cornelius' microphone off its stand. He brought it over to him.

Cornelius tentatively took it and raising himself to his knees mumbled: "Good night, Lyme Regis."

He then pushed himself up to his feet, brushing off an offer of help from his pianist. "Thanks for coming along. Hope you enjoyed the show."

He then staggered off stage, whilst the band finished off the song, including another very melodic guitar break, with a professional flourish. Then, leaving their instruments, the three stage musicians moved to the front of the stage, bowed, as one, and then followed their leader off to the wings.

The crowd cheered.

"There'll be no encore tonight," said Frank.

In a buzz of confused murmurings, people started moving slowly and haphazardly away from the sand back towards Marine Parade. Once more Ella clasped on to Frank's arm. "That was lovely. Apart from the end. I do hope he's all right."

"I'm sure he is," twinkled Frank, "Let's find ourselves a drink."

The stage lights went off and *Corn on the Cobb* was over.

# CHAPTER 4

## FOOD GLORIOUS FOOD

The pubs they attempted to enter were all jam-packed with either tourists or locals. Ella didn't like the idea of waiting around for hours to be served, so they wandered through the narrow side streets of Lyme Regis, before discovering an enterprising café providing hot drinks and snacks to the seaside visitors. The place was busy, but it was less crowded than the pubs and they managed to nab themselves a small table by the window. Frank went and ordered a pot of tea.

When he returned Ella smiled at him. "Most cafés close at six o'clock in East Devon," she remarked.

"Ah, but we're in Dorset now."

"That's what makes the difference!"

"Slip over the county border and you're in a whole new world!"

Although it was late evening, a lot of the gift shops were still open and doing roaring trade. The town was awash with visitors - families and couples wandering up and down Broad Street enjoying the holiday atmosphere.

Frank and Ella looked around the well-populated café. There was plenty of animated discussion about the unfortunate finale to the concert with the overwhelming opinion that if Cornelius couldn't stay the course, he shouldn't be still performing.

"He must be an old man now. His hits were all in the sixties."

"I bet he's worth a fortune. Why does he risk his health on a seaside summer tour?"

"I saw him last month in Margate. He collapsed at the end of the concert there as well!"

"That proves it."

There were numerous nods of agreement.

As their pot of tea arrived, Frank turned to Ella, "Remember James Brown?"

"Hardest working man in show-business?"

"Yes, that one. He often collapsed at the end of his show. It wasn't always through exhaustion or illness. It was a staged climax to the evening's show."

"He faked it? You think Cornelius did the same?"

"Hmm, it saves him doing an encore."

"Bit dramatic."

"Very dramatic but it makes sure his name is in next week's local paper."

Ella nodded and went back to people-watching outside on Broad Street.

"There she is again. And she's still with Reeves the butler."

"Who is?"

"Cornelius' wife. Shouldn't she be by her husband's side? Not with the butler."

Frank looked up from pouring the tea.

"Where are they?"

Ella began to point her out, but it was obvious that they had disappeared into the crowds.

"Gone!"

"Have a cup of tea."

After a pleasant hour of gentle conversation and people-watching, Frank and Ella ambled back to their car and headed back to the Cobb Country House Hotel. All was peaceful and they were soon getting ready for bed.

"This is a lovely place. Hushed, genteel, restrained. Just what we need after the hustle and bustle of the past few months," Ella sighed.

"It's so quiet, I'm going to open the sash window. The only disturbance will be tomorrow's dawn chorus." Frank took a while but worked out the mechanism. "It's like those old windows we used to have at school."

As Ella and Frank settled down with a Sudoku and an Agatha Christie respectively, there was a roar of a vehicle as it crunched over the gravel outside the hotel. It must have come to a halt as the engine went silent before there was a slamming of doors and some over-loud conversation.

"I 'ope the bar's still open! Rock and roll is thirsty work."

"Especially if no one even knows you were there."

"You were great tonight. Terrific solos - as usual."

"Thanks. Is the bar still open?"

"Bound to be! Mine's a cider!"

"Sowden Valley's meant to be the best around here!"

"You've done your usual research?"

"Of course!"

"OK, four pints of Sowden Valley it is!"

The hotel's front door was slammed shut and peace once more returned to the Raleigh's room.

"Was that the Portobello Crooners?"

"Crooners was perhaps the wrong name," Ella chortled. "Noisy rabble, more like!"

"I wonder if Cornelius has recovered?"

Another vehicle screeched up the drive.

"Sounds like a motor bike."

Frank slid out of the bed and stepped across to the window. He twitched through the gap in the curtains. "You were right. Now, what type of bike would an old rock and roller ride?"

"Harley Davidson?"

"Spot on the mark."

A van followed up the drive and stopped beside the Harley.

"Hey, Jimmy."

"It's Johnny, Cornelius."

"Yes, of course, it is. Have you got my bag?"

"Of course."

"Then send it up to my room. Which room am I in, Jimmy?"

"You're in the French Lieutenant's Suite."

"Largest in the hotel?"

"Of course. Dickens bed, William Holland copper bath and especially for you, Thomas Crapper toilets!"

"Great, see you next week in Plymouth. Enjoy your break!"

The van drove off, the hotel door slammed again, and Cornelius retired.

Frank returned to bed and picked up his kindle.

Ella was delighted. "Wow, Frank! The great Cornelius Spooner is staying at the same hotel as little ol' me."

"Wow, indeed!"

"You certainly picked the right hotel for our anniversary weekend! Hobnobbing with the celebrities. Perhaps we'll see him at breakfast?"

The dawn chorus didn't wake them up. Neither did the Portobello Crooners. Frank and Ella's internal body clocks woke them up at six-thirty and after a leisurely cup of tea in bed, they found their way down to breakfast at eight-thirty.

The dining room was sparkling bright and airy. The sun shone in through the French windows. The tables were arranged with immaculate white tablecloths topped with grey lacy coveralls. Silver cutlery and stylish white retro crockery adorned each table. However, the room, as yet, was empty. Frank looked at his watch. Frank and Ella went over to a long sleek mahogany table and ignoring the cereals, poured themselves a fruit drink.

"Porridge?" asked Ella.

"No, I want to leave space for a full English!"

After a few minutes, Reeves the butler appeared and took their order for cooked breakfast. "Full English breakfast with all the trimmings, please for both of us," said Ella.

"Tea or coffee, madam?"

"Tea for me."

"And for me," added Frank.

"Did we hear that Cornelius Spooner is staying here?" asked Ella.

"I'm afraid I'm not at liberty to discuss any of the other guests, madam," replied Reeves stiffly, tapping his fingers on the table.

"No, of course not! Sorry for asking."

"I'll take your order through to our chef."

The breakfast was exquisite. The conversation was superb. Frank and Ella over-indulged in both. Three guests walked into the room and helped themselves to porridge. Ella recognised them as members of the Portobello Crooners.

"We did enjoy last night," Ella smiled as she spoke.

One of the Crooners nodded at her, grunted and tucked morosely into his porridge.

"Three bears," muttered Frank, quietly enough not to be overheard. "Where's Goldilocks?"

Ella smiled once more and finished off her toast and marmalade.

The fourth member of the band appeared and stood by the mahogany table. "The unseen star of the show makes a visibly tardy entrance."

"Shut up, help yourself to porridge and sit down," groaned one of the bears.

Reeves came into the room and took orders from the four band members for breakfast. Within a couple of minutes, each of them was silently engrossed in their full English.

The room was tranquil except for the clink of cutlery and the satisfactory chomping sounds from the Crooners.

Frank folded his napkin and left it beside his plate: "Perhaps a good long walk is on the agenda today!" he laughed. "We're only a short step from the Coast Path."

"You mean to walk off all this lovely food?"

"Yes!"

"Perhaps later in the week, when we're back in the real world."

Ella was about to get up from their table when Cornelius Spooner sauntered into the room carrying a bundle of what looked like publicity photos.

"Hi, chaps! Good night, eh?"

The four band members grunted in unison, so Cornelius shrugged his shoulders and deliberately sat down at another table nearby and perused the menu. Reeves appeared by his side. He was carrying a sharp knife and wearing a distinct scowl.

"Ah, waiter. I'll have your very best cooked breakfast with no fat on the bacon, fresh mushrooms but no fried bread and definitely no hash browns. Do you know what pigs in blankets are? I'd like five of them. Did you get that? Bring me tea - not coffee. Yorkshire tea, if you have it, but under no circumstances bring me Earl Grey. Disgusting stuff."

Reeves realised he was holding the knife. As he hid it behind his back, Frank got the feeling Reeves was wondering whether he could use it for another purpose. "Certainly, sir." His fixed expression betrayed no emotion.

Cornelius looked up at him.

"Have we met before?"

"I don't know, sir, have we?"

"No, I don't think so. All you waiters look the same to me."

Reeves pivoted and left the room.

Ella looked across at Cornelius who had his back to both of them.

"He's just like a rock star. He cares for no one but himself."

"Yes," agreed Frank.

"Isn't it wonderful to be like that!"

"No, certainly not!"

Ella sat in her chair, poured herself another cup of tea and settled down for the long haul.

Ten minutes later, Reeves appeared with the tea pot in one hand and hot water jug in the other. Cornelius was busily scribbling away on the photos.

"Yorkshire, sir."

"But, of course. Well done. Now, where's my breakfast?"

Ella was enjoying the entertainment. Reeves stared impassively and left the room. Frank noticed that this time there was no knife.

After a short while, Reeves re-appeared with the breakfast.

"You took your time. I've nearly completed these autographs. For the fans, you know. They love the personal touch. Handled by a pop star." He looked around at the room.

"Everyone else has nearly finished."

"Sir's specific requirements had to be explained to our chef, sir."

"Right, well, he'd better have got it right. And, I hope you haven't added any saliva."

Reeves' face imperceptibly changed colour. Ella almost giggled out loud. One of the Crooners looked up and raised his eyebrows.

"Because if you did, I'd sue the lot of you, and you'd never work in hospitality ever again."

"Sir, the thought never crossed my mind. We are an establishment that prides itself on our customer care in all circumstances."

"Glad to hear it."

Cornelius began to attack his food but abruptly stopped.

"Oi, waiter. Take these photos with my autograph on them and put them in reception. My tour manager will pick them up at some point later in the week."

"Certainly, sir. Your wish..."

"Yeah, is my command. Now clear off and let me eat in peace."

After a short while, he turned towards the Crooners and waving his knife in the air said, "Good grub, this. We struck lucky with this place."

He took another mouthful of Dorset sausage before resuming.

"Beats some of the places I was forced to stay in back in the sixties."

He dipped another chunk of sausage into his fried egg.

"Of course, you youngsters wouldn't remember that far back. You get it too easy these days. I'm paying you far too much." Cornelius burped without apology.

Ella was truly smitten by the gross manners of this man.

Frank admired both Reeves and the Crooners for their fortitude.

As Cornelius was finishing his meal, the lady from the garden, the wife of Cornelius, walked in through the main dining room door and sat down near the Crooners.

Cornelius looked up. A frown creased his forehead and waving his knife in the air once again, he muttered "Don't I know you?"

And then the mist cleared.

"It's Diane, isn't it? Hello darling, good to see you again. It must be years. What are you doing here?"

"I thought you invited me?"

"What? You're confusing me. I don't understand?"

"Someone sent me a letter," Diane remarked.

"Not from me. I don't write letters. Gave that up years ago. I get my manager to do all that sort of stuff."

"Perhaps he wrote it on your behalf?"

"No, I don't think so." Cornelius took a chair from an adjacent table. "Come and sit here. Join me for some breakfast."

He looked across at the band members.

"My band don't seem to want to be with their leader."

"We're off for a walk, Cornie. Want to join us?"

"It's Cornelius, you young whippersnapper. Hey, come and join me," he directed his comments at Diane.

She thought about it for a moment and then got up from her chair and moved over to Cornelius' table.

"Now what do you want to eat? Full English? Looks like you need it."

Diane nodded, and sat down, still unsure of the situation.

"Oi, waiter!" Cornelius shouted. "Service!"

After a gap of about fifteen seconds, Reeves appeared with a quizzical look on his face. He stood by the table in silence. His only concession to an outward appearance of annoyance was a slight rhythmic tapping of one foot.

"Ah, there you are. Full English breakfast for this lady. And bring coffee and some more tea. And while you're at it, more toast and marmalade. This could take some time. We've got a lot of catching up to do."

# CHAPTER 5

# ROLL OUT THE BARREL

Frank and Ella sat there enjoying the evolving spectacle.

"What wonderful entertainment," whispered Ella.

"I think it's time we left."

"Spoilsport."

Frank dabbed his lips with his napkin before placing it on his plate. He stood up and moved around the table behind Ella. He held and moved her chair as she raised herself gracefully to her feet.

"Thank you, kind sir." Ella smiled adoringly at Frank before following him out of the dining room and up to their room.

Frank looked out of the window. "The weather's glorious. Let's go for a walk."

Ella frowned. "Just around the garden and maybe down to the sea. Nothing too strenuous."

"OK."

"Maybe a wander around Lyme Regis this afternoon?"

The hotel garden dazzled under a clear blue sky and the pleasant warmth of the morning sun. Fuscias and hydrangeas dominated the borders of the pristine lawns.

As they ambled around the side of the hotel, Frank spied someone stooped over the dustbins.

"Well, that's strange. A woman is rummaging through the hotel dustbins. Don't they feed the staff properly at this hotel?"

Ella turned to look and shouted, "Excuse me, can we help you?"

The middle-aged woman disguised her attractiveness with an old-patterned coat and a knitted woollen hat. She stopped her foraging and turned towards them.

Ella asked, "Are you with the band?"

Frank smiled. "Cornelius Spooner and the Portobello Crooners?"

"Of course, who else." The woman approached them with an expectant look on her face. "And you're not Albert Hamm, the drummer?"

"Er no."

"No, you don't look anything like him. Unless he's been sacked? No, Cornelius wouldn't sack him- he's too good. He's the best drummer the Crooners have ever had. Mind you, if they'd held on to Dave Clark."

"The Dave Clark? From the Dave Clark Five?"

"Yeah, the rumour was that Cornelius employed the Dave Clark Five before they became famous. They were from Tottenham and he was from Ladbroke Grove. Of course, North London and West London don't mix. Different cultures. They played a few gigs together and then had some sort of argument and they all left. That happened all the time in the sixties. Although, obviously, I'm far too young to have seen him back then."

"Obviously," echoed Ella.

"There was a time when he changed his band every tour. Sometimes for the better, sometimes for the worse. It didn't stop Cornelius from being the star. Nothing would stop Cornelius from being the star. Did you see him last night? Wasn't he fab? I think that was his best performance of the tour so far. I've seen every concert on this year's tour. He just seems to get better and better!"

Frank attempted to stop the flow. "Are you staying at the hotel?"

"No, I couldn't afford places like this every night. I'm in a cheap B&B in Lyme Regis. I popped up here on the bus."

"What were you doing around the dustbins?"

"Oh, wasn't it obvious?"

"No," replied Ella.

"You were following in the footsteps of the Dylanologists, weren't you?" guessed Frank.

"Eh? Sorry, don't understand."

"In the sixties, fans of Bob Dylan used to raid his dustbins looking for anything that could give a greater understanding of his genius. Scraps of paper with discarded lyrics. Food remains."

"Food remains?" Ella queried.

"Yes, some people thought that he must be eating a special diet to be able to produce such creative work."

"I don't know who Dylanologists are, but you're on the right tracks. I was just looking for anything from Cornelius Spooner. Over the years I've built up a collection of mementoes and souvenirs. Sometime in the future, it'll be worth a fortune. Not that I'm ever going to sell it! I've got last night's poster and my ticket, of course. And I took loads of photos. And I recorded his act as usual. But it'd be great to find a special souvenir-

something different and unique."

The lady stopped to catch her breath.

"Well, there's some autographed photos of Cornelius on the front desk in reception."

"Nah, they're not unique. Two a penny."

The lady thought about resuming her foraging but then seemed to remember her manners.

"Oops, I haven't even introduced myself. I'm Annie Saxon. Cornelius Spooner's number one fan!"

Ella went to shake hands. Annie's wedding ring glinted in the sun, but her hands were filthy and still holding some of the bin rubbish.

"Oh, better not." Annie raised her hands. "Don't know what might have been thrown in those dustbins!"

Ella withdrew her hands and put them firmly in her pockets.

"Did you find anything?"

Annie put the rubbish back into the bins and wiped her hands on her coat.

"No, it's a bit early in the day. I'll go back later on when the staff have had a chance to do some housework! Oh, by the way, do you know which room he's staying in? It's bound to be one of the most expensive suites. Nothing's too good for my Cornelius."

"I'm afraid not. We saw him at breakfast, but that's all."

"At breakfast. What did he have?"

"Tea and a full English, I think. He was talking to a woman. Someone from a long time ago."

"A woman!" Annie looked aghast.

"Yes, we met her yesterday. I seem to remember her saying she was his wife."

"Which one?"

"She didn't say."

"Did she stay with him in his room?"

"I don't think so. He had a bit of trouble remembering her."

"Then that's OK." Annie stood there as if lost in thought. "Could you do me a favour?"

"Well, I'm not so sure."

"Could you smuggle me into the hotel? I'll find his room number and see if I can get a few minutes with him."

Ella was about to let her down gently when she noticed Reeves the butler making his way towards them.

"Excuse me, sir and madam. Is this lady bothering you?"

"Er, well...."

"I'm just going. I was out for a walk and I lost my way. This kind couple has given me directions back to the coast path. Many thanks."

Annie went to turn away towards the front of the hotel. As she did, she turned back to Reeves.

"Don't I know you? Haven't I seen you somewhere before?"

"I expect so, madam. A butler turns up in so many different places."

Annie walked away from them, around the side of the hotel, and out of their view.

Reeves rhythmically tapped his foot. "I do apologise for that interruption. We don't normally suffer from the riff-raff."

"She seemed friendly."

"Yes, too friendly. I expect it's because we have that group of so-called musicians staying here."

"Yes, they made a bit of noise last night, didn't they?"

"I do apologise. I hope it hasn't spoilt your stay?"

"No, not a problem, replied Ella.

Annie had disappeared down the drive and through the gates.

"She was an interesting character. She says that she's Cornelius Spooner's number one fan."

"Aren't they all, madam, aren't they all?"

Frank and Ella continued into the garden. It was a gloriously sunny morning. Over by the archery gallery they watched one of the band members practising.

"That's not a guitar!"

"Even I can see that," replied Frank. "It's a crossbow. And, if I'm not mistaken, he's the off-stage guitarist."

"Hello," cried Ella as they approached. "Please don't shoot!"

The youngster smiled, put down his crossbow and came across to them.

"I thought your guitar playing last night was excellent," said Frank.

"Thanks, I'm glad someone noticed."

"Couldn't help but notice. Especially as Cornelius' guitar wasn't plugged in!"

"Yes, just a little trick of mine. Some people notice and they look for the real guitarist rather than the fakester."

"Yes, I'm sure you've got a great future. What's your name so that I can tell my grandchildren that I met the great....?"

"Johnny. Johnny Toogood."

"Is that your real name?"

"Yes, I know people think I pinched it off Johnny B Goode, but it's my real name. It's an ancient name. Goes back to before the Norman Conquest. The Toogoods of Hertfordshire. That's where we originate from. We're even in the Domesday Book. Only then it was spelt as Thurgod!"

"Nice to have met you. Enjoy your crossbow practice."

"Thanks. I've just bought it. Fortunately, there's one of the staff who's quite an expert and he showed me the basics."

He swirled the crossbow around. Frank and Ella both instinctively ducked.

"Sorry. This is my first attempt at putting his coaching into practice. I'm struggling to even reach the target at the moment."

"Well, we'll leave you to get to grips with it."

Frank and Ella carried on their gentle saunter around the garden.

"When we've completed our circuit of the garden, let's cross the road and explore down to the coast path."

"Maybe," responded Ella." Although, at the moment, I feel like being a little bit lazy."

As they reached the maze, they met Cornelius' breakfast companion sitting on a well-worn timber bench.

"Hello, that looks comfortable," said Ella. "Oh, I do like your cardigan. What a lovely vibrant colour."

"Thank you, I love orange. Sit down, do join me."

There was plenty of space so both Frank and Ella sat down. Ella smiled: "It's Diane, Diane Spooner, isn't it?"

"Yes, it is Diane. But it's Diane *Streamer* now. I went back to my maiden name. But how did you know?"

"I heard Cornelius mention your name at breakfast. We met you yesterday before *Corn on the Cobb*."

"Ah, yes, in the lounge." Diane paused. "Sorry, I'm in my

own little world. I'm just trying to figure out what's going on."

"How do you mean?" asked Frank.

"Well, I was invited down to Cobb Country House Hotel. I assumed it was by Cornelius. I was surprised - to say the least. We haven't seen each other for years. No Christmas cards, telephone calls, nothing."

"Did he say why you were invited?"

"No. He was as lambasted as me. He phoned his manager, spoke to his band and none of them knew anything about it. The band didn't even know who I was. They're too young to remember."

"Strange."

"Yes, but Cornelius did say he was so glad to see me. He gave me the old soft soap story about me being his first true love and how life had never been the same since I left. Oh, it was all sentimental clap-trap, but I got the feeling he was convincing himself that he was really uttering the truth."

"Did he convince you?"

"No, I remember the good times, of course. But there were plenty of bad times as well. He had the roving eye. In those days, that was par for the course, but it still hurt. I've never really forgiven him for that."

"Did he plead with you that he had changed?" Frank asked with the beginnings of a smile on his face.

"No, he was too busy spouting on about the old days. He never mentioned how he felt now."

Diane stared off into the distance.

"Oh, and another thing."

"Yes?"

"Sitting in the lounge, I saw Reeves, the butler. He

reminded me of someone from years back. But it couldn't be him."

Diane's voice drifted off once more as if she were transporting herself back in time.

"They told me he'd died. He ran off, Cornelius said, at the time, it was with some floozy. Died in a car accident. He was an incredible drummer. Maybe the best. But, no, it may be decades ago but…"

Frank gently sought to bring her back to the present day. "We saw you with Reeves in Lyme Regis at *Corn on the Cobb*."

"Yes, he came up to me in the crowd. I was trying to decide whether to go backstage and greet Cornelius, but Reeves, quite rightly, told me not to bother."

"After Cornelius' dramatic stage exit, we walked around for a bit and then came back to the hotel."

"Did you tell Reeves about the drummer from the past?"

"No, it would have been very rude of me. Anyway, it couldn't be him. His name wasn't Reeves. And why would a brilliant drummer be working as a butler in a country yokel hotel?"

"Why indeed?" mused Ella.

"Excuse me, I must go indoors. I'm meeting Cornelius for morning coffee."

Diane got up and floated away.

"Well, you know the saying 'The past is another country'?"

"Don't you mean 'The past is a foreign country'? LP Hartley's The Go-Between, I believe."

"Wow, you didn't even need your mobile phone search

function for that little snippet."

"The brain's still functioning. The man's still got it!" Frank performed his version of a Cheshire Cat grin.

"Careful, the door to our room isn't that wide."

"Anyway, you were saying?"

"The past, whatever. Poor Diane was swept back to another time and place. Did she really want to go there?"

"Well, I hope that's the biggest mystery we encounter this weekend. Let's get some coffee."

Frank and Ella wandered into the lounge where Reeves was serving coffee. Frank stood in front of an antique Welsh Dresser.

"Morning again, Reeves. What a beautiful piece of furniture," he said. "And look, Ella, a beer barrel."

On the middle shelf stood a miniature beer barrel, highly polished in tan-brown wood with four silver bands holding the barrel together.

"May I pick it up?" asked Frank.

"Be my guest, sir," replied Reeves as he handed a cup of coffee to Ella, "Milk and sugar, sir?"

"Just milk, please."

Frank picked up the beer barrel and rolled it along his fingers. On the side was a maker's mark.

"Well, I never, it's a Kennaway barrel."

Ella leaned over to look. "The ornate K?"

"Yes, and underneath, on the bottom. Yes, OSM."

"Ottery St Mary!"

"What's that doing here? I never knew we made miniatures."

"We, sir?" interrupted Reeves.

"Yes, Kennaway Coopers is our company."

Reeves nodded respectfully.

Ella had taken the barrel from Frank and was further inspecting the cask.

"Look here, Spooner's. You can just about read it. It says Spooner's."

"It must be a company or a brewery."

At that moment, Ella noticed that Cornelius and Diane were sitting on a sofa on the far side of the room.

"Did I hear you say Spooner's?" Cornelius boomed.

"Yes, do you own a brewery?"

"No such luck. Would I be sitting here if I did? Let me have a look."

Cornelius came over and took the miniature away from Ella.

"Well, I never. What a lark."

He tossed it in the air as if it were a tennis ball.

"How much do you want for it?" he asked turning to Ella.

"It's not ours. It belongs to the Hotel. We found it here on the Dresser."

Cornelius lobbed it back to Ella who caught it and placed it carefully in its place on the middle shelf.

"Well, Reeves. How much?"

"I'm certain that it's *not* for sale. The items on the dresser are an integral part of the ambience of this establishment."

"Yeah, whatever. How much? Everything has a price."

"Not *every*thing, sir."

"Listen, if I want something, I normally get it. Where's

the manager?"

"The manager, sir, is not available this weekend. He has placed me in charge. I am authorised to make decisions."

"Good. Then how much?"

"The item is *not* for sale, sir."

"That's ridiculous," fumed Cornelius. "It's only a miniature beer barrel."

"Indeed, sir, but it's still *not* for sale."

"What if I just come down to the lounge in the middle of the night and just pinch it? You can't stop me."

"No, sir, but if it goes missing, we'll know where to look for it."

"Aaargh," seethed Cornelius, "I'm going for a walk around the grounds."

He turned back to Diane.

"Coming?"

"Let me finish my coffee and I'll catch you up."

Cornelius stomped out of the room. Ella and Frank took their coffees and sat by the window. Frank opened the window to let some of the sunny morning air into the room as Reeves wheeled out the squeaky coffee trolley. A couple of minutes later, Diane finished her drink, nodded surreptitiously to Frank and Ella and quietly left the room for her rendezvous with Cornelius.

*Ah, there she is.*

*Where's she going?*

*Oh, this is going to be too easy. Just stay there, little lady.*

*Just stay by the well.*

*Yes, have a look down and see how deep it is.*

*Right, concentrate.*

*Gloves on?*
*Tie at the ready?*
*Calling card at the ready?*
*Don't worry, little lady.*
*Don't you just love how gullible they are?*
*You won't feel a thing. Well, not much anyway.*
*A little scream and the deed is done.*
*Sweet dreams.*
*Drum roll, please. Pussy's in the well.*

# CHAPTER 6

# DING DONG BELL

"He's got a bit a temper," reflected Ella.

"Yes, wouldn't want to be on the wrong side of Cornelius Spooner."

Frank murmured: "I wonder if we've got any more miniatures back at Kennaway Coopers?"

"Yes, we might have a spare Spooner's lying around somewhere."

"Let's not think about that now. We said, 'no shop talk' this weekend."

"Yes, you're right. Sorry!"

Peace and quiet descended upon the room and they both sat in companionable and comfortable silence sipping their coffee and enjoying the long-awaited inactivity.

A sudden breeze fluttered the curtains and brought an abrupt chill into the room.

"Perhaps you'd better shut the window, dear," Ella proposed.

As Frank got up, there was a scream from outside.

"That sounded nasty," remarked Frank. He closed the window and resumed his position and his inactivity.

"Leave it, Frank. Just another little mystery that has nothing to do with us!"

Frank and Ella enjoyed the peace and tranquility of the lounge and decided to forego their exploration beyond the main road. Time passed sedately and all too soon it was lunch. They heard the gong reverberating in the reception area, so, slowly and reluctantly, they both rose from the sofa, stretched and made their way to the dining room.

The dining room was filling up. The four members of the band were already seated, and a grumpy looking Cornelius stumped in and sat on his own looking out over the gardens. Frank and Ella occupied a table near the door which provided them with an unrestricted view of the other diners.

A waitress, a young girl who looked as if she was still attending school, walked in and handed out a menu to each table.

As she reached Frank and Ella's table she looked around as if she were counting the diners. "I was told there'd be two ladies. Where's the other?"

Ella quickly surveyed the scene and noticed Diane had not yet arrived. "I'm sure she'll be here in a minute."

Frank and Ella ordered the soup followed by the Sunday roast and settled down to enjoy their meal.

The four Portobello Crooners chatted amicably between themselves whilst Cornelius, on his own table, appeared to be sulking whilst facing away from everyone else.

The soup was appetisingly delicious, the roast up to the standard of typical Westcountry fare and all was well with the world.

As they finished their roast, they sat back wondering whether they dare contemplate one of the puddings from the menu. Cornelius stood up and approached their table. "Here," he croaked in a stage whisper, "did you see what happened to Diane?"

"Wasn't she joining you in the garden?" Ella replied.

"Yeah, that's what I thought. But she never turned up. Typical woman!"

"So where is she?" asked Frank.

"I thought you'd know."

"Well, she left the lounge a couple of minutes after you did. We assumed she was catching you up."

"She never did. I waited for her by the maze, but she never turned up. I got fed up waiting for her, so I went into the maze. It took forever to get out again."

Cornelius turned to the Crooners.

"Here, did any of you clap eyes on Diane?"

All four shook their heads.

"Then where, in heaven's name, is she?"

Reeves appeared at the door.

"Oi, have you seen the lady who was with me in the coffee room?"

"Are you referring to your first wife, sir?"

"Diane. Yeah, that's the one."

There was a pause.

"Well, have you seen her?"

"No, sir. I would have responded positively to your original query if I had."

"Then, I repeat, where, in heaven's name, is she?"

"Perhaps she's gone for a walk, boss," ventured Johnny.

"But it's lunchtime."

"She'll be back when her stomach starts rumbling."

"Thanks, Johnny, for your heartfelt concern."

"Just saying, boss. Wait a while and she'll be back."

They waited awhile. At around four o'clock, Johnny Toogood found Ella and Frank in the lounge. "I've got a nasty feeling about this. The boss looks terrible. I thought we were going to have a rehearsal of a couple of new songs for next week, but he's scotched that idea. He seems very worried."

"Do you want us to form a search party?" asked Frank.

"Exactly!"

"So where do we start?"

Johnny shook his head in a questioning manner. Ella went to the window and opened it.

She turned around to Frank. "Remember you heard a scream this morning? What if...."

"No, don't be so morbid."

"It's worth checking."

"Yes, I suppose it won't do any harm." He turned back to the guitarist and would be crossbowman. "Johnny, we heard a scream this morning before lunch. Perhaps we ought to start in hearing range of this window."

The three of them walked outside and assembled in front of the still-open window. "Look around, are there any places in sight that could cause a person to scream?"

Frank pointed at some trees and bushes to their right. "Someone could have fallen or tripped and be lying there without anyone else seeing them."

"They could be unconscious," added Johnny.

They moved towards the trees and spent ten minutes

searching through the bushes to no avail. "No, she's not here."

"Where else?"

They moved across the gardens keeping approximately the same distance away from the lounge windows. Ahead of them was the medieval well. The wooden circular slab top was lying on the grass nearby.

"That should be on top of the well," remarked Frank.

"Oh no, please, not in there," uttered Ella.

They approached it and stood by not wanting to be the first to look down the well.

"The moss around the edge has been scuffed," observed Frank.

"Who's going to look?" Johnny thought that if he voiced the action then somebody would put the action into practice.

No-one moved.

"Oh, all right, I'll do it." He approached the edge of the well and down into the depths.

"What can you see?"

"It's deep and dark and… oh no. There's something or somebody down there!"

"Excuse me, can I help?" Reeves had silently approached them and sternly addressed the three of them.

"Yes, you can phone the fire brigade. Oh, and the police," Ella ordered.

"Pardon, madam?"

"There's a body in the well."

"Probably left over from Guy Fawkes night last year. I heard someone say they had too many guys and threw one away. I bet that's where it went."

"I don't think so," said Ella. "Are you going to phone the

fire brigade and the police?"

Reeves stood there tapping one foot rhythmically on the gravel around the well. "No, Madam, I am not. I have the reputation of the Cobb Country House Hotel to consider. The other lady will turn up soon."

"Not if she's fallen into the well."

"Look, we're wasting time. I'll go and get my phone and call them myself!" sighed Frank.

He walked away back towards the hotel. "It's in our room. I won't be long."

Ella crossed her arms and stood still. "I'm not moving from here until Frank gets back. We don't want anyone tampering with the evidence. After all, we have the reputation of the Cobb Country House Hotel to consider!"

Reeves silently withdrew looking nonplussed. "I don't think he's used to being over-ruled," muttered Ella to herself.

"Oh no, not you again!" Sergeant Elsie Knowle emerged from the police car with a mock look of horror on her face.

"It's Frank. Hi!" PC Alf Hydon greeted him with a sense of genuine enthusiasm, "Fancy seeing you here! Where's Ella!"

"Guarding the body."

"Right, take us there then. Any time I attend a suspicious death in East Devon, there's a good chance you'll be there as well."

Frank led the way to the well.

"At least this one's not stuck in a barrel."

"No, down a well!"

"Great, have you been down in a bucket to search for clues?"

"No, there wasn't a bucket handy!"

PC Alf Hydon chuckled in delight.

Sergeant Knowle stopped and turned to her colleague. "May I remind you that we are here in a professional capacity!"

"Sorry, ma'am. Yes, ma'am. My notebook is at the ready."

They reached the well. A small crowd of employees and guests had gathered around the well. Ella still stood guard, arms crossed, keeping all onlookers a suitable distance away from the well.

"Hello, Ella. Thank you for preventing the tampering of any evidence. We'll take over from here!"

Ella uncrossed her arms and stood aside.

Sergeant Knowle put one gloved hand on the edge of the well and stared down into the depths.

"Yes, there's something down there. Looks like a body. And there are scuff marks on the edge here." Realising she could be contaminating the evidence, she quickly withdrew her gloved hand and turned to PC Hydon. "Could you take photos of the rim of the well and the surrounding land before the scene of crime people mess it up? We'll also need the Fire Brigade.

"We've already called them," Frank chipped in, "Same time as you."

"They'll be here soon then."

PC Hydon had taken out his phone and was busy snapping the aforementioned area. When he had finished, he moved everyone back from the scene. He then secured it with police tape and some poles retrieved from the police car.

"I could try climbing down the well. 'E's not too deep. I could try out my waterproof pen or me wi-fi whistle."

"No, PC Hydon, no. Just move these people back so we can conduct an orderly investigation." Alf sighed and then turned to those gathered around.

"Right, ladees and gennelmen, step back. Oi'd like you all to walk back to the hotel and wait in …"

"The dining room?" suggested Ella.

"Indeed, the dining room until we're ready to speak to you."

Some of the crowd moved slowly away.

"All of you. Now, please! Thank 'ee. You as well, Mr. and Mrs. Raleigh. This is police business now."

Frank and Ella joined the group in the dining room. There were the four band members, the waitress from lunchtime, a man dressed in a butcher's apron who Ella assumed was the chef, Cornelius and Reeves. Also, sitting in the corner, to Ella's surprise was Annie Saxon, the dustbin woman.

Everyone found a chair to sit down in. The atmosphere was different to that of breakfast this morning. The chatter and brashness seemed a world away. It had been replaced by an appreciably dark tension in the room.

Frank sat with Ella near the window. Frank gazed around the room before whispering in Ella's ear, "Look at them all. Some look scared, some trying to make it seem as if they couldn't care less, others bursting with curiosity and excitement."

"So much for a quiet relaxing weekend without any mystery," murmured Ella back to him.

"What do you mean?"

"Well, one of them, unless I'm very much mistaken...

may be a murderer."

The fire brigade took their time in arriving. "Sorry," said the lead fireman. "We were at another call. Came as soon as we could."

By using something that looked like a winch balanced on a tripod, one of the smaller firemen was lowered into the well. Half an hour later, after a lot of earnest discussions, a body was carefully raised back onto solid ground. Frank had chosen his seat specifically so that he could look out of the window into the garden.

The body was muddied and broken. Frank glimpsed a remnant of orange clothing.

"It's her," he breathed to Ella.

"How do you know?"

"Orange, I can see orange."

As the Fire Brigade left, PC Hydon took photos and made measurements. He coated the rim of the well for fingerprints before the ambulance took away the body. Inspector Wilkins arrived from Exeter. He was not a favourite of either Elsie or Alf.

"Right then, WPC Knowles. Oh, I see from your uniform you've been promoted. *Sergeant* Knowles. Fill me in on the circumstances of this accident."

"Yes sir. We are not sure, but we *think* that this may be a murder case. The evidence is leading us to think that the body may have been pushed down the well. We think the murderer may be someone still on the premises."

"Thank you, Sergeant Knowles. Unfortunately for you,

you are not paid to think but simply inform me of the facts. I'll decide if it was an accident or murder."

"It's Sergeant Knowle, sir," interrupted PC Hydon.

"I'm very well aware of whom I am conversing with. Haven't you got some crowd controlling to do? Go and stand by the gates and keep the crowd under control."

"There's nobody at the gate."

"Well, go and see if the guests and staff are OK. They're our customers. Go and care for them. That's not too difficult a task, is it?"

Alf stood there, not used to being spoken to in that manner.

"Well go on, off with you!"

PC Hydon retreated from the scene with commendable restraint.

"I hope he's not too much of a thorn in your side, Sergeant Knowles."

"No sir, he's not usually that obstreperous."

"Good. I want your report on my desk in the morning. I will decide whether this accident needs further investigation. You follow procedure and make sure the general public is not inconvenienced by your presence."

Inspector Wilkins turned away and waddled back to his car.

"Good evening, sir."

"Yes, yes, whatever."

The inspector left the scene of the crime. Sergeant Knowle found a quiet place in the hotel to write up her report.

It took another hour and a half before Sergeant Knowle appeared in the dining room.

"Sorry to have kept you. Can someone go into the kitchen and make all of us some tea and coffee? Bring out some biscuits as well. PC Hydon here will help you."

"I'm glad to get rid of Alf for a while. He's on a new gadget craze. If it's not his wi-fi police whistle, it's his sticky tracker or his tactical waterproof pen. He's desperate to try them all!"

Ten minutes later everyone was furnished with tea or coffee and a selection of Devon biscuits.

Hardly anyone spoke except those who said thank you as the refreshments were handed out.

"Right, let me tell you what is going on." Sergeant Knowle stood by the window blocking out the view of the outside activities.

"We've retrieved a body from the well, a dead body." There was a gasp around the room. The waitress who was sat near Ella was obviously on the verge of tears. Ella reached out and grasped her hand. Tears silently rolled down her face.

"It's Diane, isn't it?" said Frank.

"We're not in a position to identify her yet."

"She was wearing a vivid orange cardigan," Frank continued. Ella nodded.

"Thank you, Mr. Raleigh. PC Hydon put down your cup of tea and find her room."

"She was in the Monmouth Room," the waitress volunteered.

"Thank you, miss."

"Mister Reeves will have the master swipe-card."

"Thank you once again. Which one of you is Mister Reeves?"

Reeves stood and extracted the master swipe-card from

his jacket pocket. "Shall I go with the policeman, madame?"

"No, that won't be necessary. Please take your seat again."

Reeves sat down and PC Hydon took the swipe-card and left the room.

"Now, in the next couple of hours, we're going to be asking each one of you some questions. It is in your best interests to answer every question truthfully. You will stay here until you have answered the questions and then you may go to your rooms. I assume all the staff live in?"

The waitress put her hand up. "No, miss, I live in the village. Rousdon. My mum and dad will be expecting me home at about this time."

"OK, we'll deal with you first and then I'll ring your parents and ask them to come and collect you."

"My sister works as the receptionist here and she's waiting for me in that group on the driveway."

PC Hydon moved towards the dining-room door. "Ma'am, I'll patrol the front gate. Just in case we get outsiders wandering in."

"Good idea, PC Hydon."

He was already gone.

"Now, is there a room we can use?"

Reeves once more stood up. "The lounge, ma'am. Across the hall."

"Excellent, the lounge it is. The rest of you stay here, except you, Mrs. Raleigh."

Ella let go of the girl's hand, wiped her tears away and stood up. "Me?"

"Yes, in the absence of a WPC, you'll have to witness that my questions are fair and not intrusive."

Ella, the waitress and Sergeant Knowle left the room.

# CHAPTER 7

# MORE QUESTIONS THAN ANSWERS

Ella led the way out of the dining room and past reception to the lounge. At the reception desk stood a lady just about to ring the service bell.

Sergeant Knowle stopped, looked at her and asked, "Excuse me, can I help you?"

"Yes, I'd like to book in, find my room and have a good long bath. It's been a harrying journey."

"How did you get past the policeman at the gate?"

"He let me in when I told him I was a guest staying at the hotel."

Sergeant Knowle looked fit to explode. "Don't you realise you have walked straight into a potential murder scene?"

"Well, that's got nothing to do with me. I just want a bath."

"Shall I register her and show her to her room?" asked the waitress.

"Yes, but be quick. Ella, would you go with her, please?

I'll wait in the lounge."

"She'll be in the Somers room."

Five minutes later, the guest was signed in and Ella and the waitress joined Sergeant Knowle in the lounge.

"Right, before we start, let's get some names sorted out. Who was our new arrival?"

"She says she's come down from Northampton. Mary registered her and I left her having a bath in her en-suite. I've told her not to leave her room until Mary, here, or Reeves, fetches her."

"Good, thank you, Ella."

"Perhaps we need to find out more about her?"

We will but all in good time. So," Sergeant Knowle said turning to her first interviewee, "You're Mary?"

"Yes, Mary Maynard. I live in the village and my older sister, Martha, is waiting with the group of other villagers out by the gates."

"Thank you. We won't keep you too long. This is Ella Raleigh. She's helped us out before, and I have every confidence in her. I trust her and I'm sure, you will too!"

Ella felt herself starting to blush.

"Now, I'm Elsie but I am known as Sergeant Knowle. You can call me Elsie if that makes you feel more comfortable. Now tell me, have you met the deceased this weekend?"

"Yes, her name was Diane Streamer. I signed her in and showed her to her room."

"Did you serve her in the dining room?"

"No, I don't do breakfasts and she didn't turn up for her dinner."

"When did you realise there was something wrong?"

"Well, after lunch I was on reception duty. I had been

there all afternoon until I heard a bit of a kerfuffle when they discovered her body in the well." Mary looked at Ella, "Your husband ran past me and shouted something like 'I need my phone.' A couple of minutes later he returned and told me the police and fire brigade would be arriving soon and not to let anyone near the garden."

"So, what did you do?"

"Well, I'm sorry. I didn't really understand what he meant so I went out to the garden to see what was going on."

"And what *was* going on?"

"I saw Ella, Mrs. Raleigh, her husband and Reeves standing around the well."

"Nobody else?"

"No, not at first. Emanuel, the chef, came out a while later and stood with me. I tried to explain what was going on but he doesn't speak English very well - he's from Barcelona."

Ella resisted the urge to laugh.

"Then one by one, the guests seemed to materialise. Like bees around a honey pot. Strangely, they all came from different directions and they were all on their own."

"Did you see Diane Streamer leave the hotel?"

"When?"

"Sometime before lunch," Ella interrupted.

"No, I wasn't in Reception. I was in the kitchen helping the chef. You don't see much of the outside world in the kitchen."

"Who was at Reception?"

"Well, it should have been Reeves, but he gets called away to deal with all sorts of other matters, so it could have been unmanned."

"Thank you, Mary. Is there anything else you'd like to add?"

"No, I've told you all I've seen. Can I go home now?"

"Yes, are you working any other times this week?"

"No, but my sister, Martha, is. All week. It's the school holidays and she's allowed to work here during the holidays. Will it be safe?"

"Yes, I think she'll be perfectly safe. If you have any further worries, or if you or your sister see or hear anything of interest then let Ella here know all about it. Thank you for your excellent interview."

Ella got up and opened the door for Mary. She smiled, left the room and headed straight for the front door of the hotel. Ella could hear her cry "Martha!!" as she ran down the drive.

Ella went back into the lounge. Elsie was standing by the window "So who have we got who might tell us more?"

"I thought she told us a lot," replied Ella. "What about going to the heart of the matter and interviewing Cornelius Spooner?"

"Why do you say that?"

"Well, he's the most obvious suspect. Diane Streamer was his first wife. Maybe she was after his money and Cornelius can be a bit quick-tempered. I'd like to know where he was."

"And I'd like to know who Betty Brook-Spooner is. A relative? Another wife?"

"Let's interview Cornelius. This time I'd like Frank in here as well. Give us the male perspective. This is not an official interview. We are just gathering information. Nothing says we can't have two civilians involved. You sit here. I'll go and get the two of them."

It was some time before Elsie returned with Cornelius

and Frank.

"Please sit down, Mr. Spooner. This is just a bit of information gathering. Trying to find out where everyone was and what they saw."

"Yeah, I understand. Why are these two here?"

"To bring a bit of perspective to the proceedings. Making sure I don't overstep the mark. They've done this sort of thing before. Do you mind?"

"No, I've got nothing to hide."

"Do you know who the deceased was?"

"Well, if it's Diane, then yes - she was my first wife."

"Diane Streamer?"

"That what she calls herself now- it was her maiden name."

"Tell me about her."

"We were too young when we met. We married too young. We split up too young. I was off around the country singing and enjoying myself. Surrounded by adoring fans. She was stuck at home. One day she'd had enough and scarpered off to her mum. I tried to talk to her, but her mum wouldn't hear of it. We got a quiet divorce. Most of my fans didn't even know I was married."

"I assume you invited her down here for old times sake?"

"No, that's just it. I was as surprised as anybody to see her here. It took me a few minutes to work out where I'd seen her before. I didn't invite her and neither did Henry."

"Henry?"

"Henry Soames, my manager."

"Which one is he? In the dining room?"

"None of them. He's not here. He had to go back to

London to deal with some business matters. He'll be back on the tour next weekend. We're due to play Plymouth. This week is meant to be a rest week. We're here till Friday. It's our mid-tour treat. Fine treat, it's turning out to be!"

Frank butted in. "Didn't you meet Diane in the gardens after coffee?"

"Well, we were meant to. But she never turned up. Now I know why."

"Pardon?"

"Some geezer stuffed her down that well out there. If I find out, who did it, you'll have to arrest me as well - for murdering a murderer!"

"So, you don't think it was an accident?"

"Accident? Never thought of that. You'd have to be a bit dippy to fall down a well, *accidentally*!!"

"And was she, er, dippy?"

"Yeah, she could be. Certainly, back in the day..."

"Some people might wonder, Mr. Spooner," Elsie resumed the questioning, "whether you did meet her, and she demanded money off you. You got angry and pushed her down the well."

"Well, some people would be completely and utterly wrong."

Elsie raised an eyebrow.

"I liked her, hell, I loved her. I loved all my wives. They may have tried to fleece me, but I wouldn't kill them. I've done my share of, shall we say, ill-advised deeds in the past but killing ain't one of them!"

"Where were you before and after lunch?"

"In the garden. I sat down by the maze and just took in the quiet. I don't get too much of that!"

"Who was with you?"

"Nobody. Before lunch, I was waiting for Diane, but she never arrived. After lunch, I needed my own space."

"Thank you, Mr. Spooner. I'm sure we'll speak to you again. Maybe, more formally."

"Yeah, yeah, whatever. I repeat. I've got nothing to hide. I'll be in my room if you need me."

Cornelius got up and left.

Frank nodded to himself. "Well, he seemed genuine. I didn't detect any *obvious* lies."

Elsie turned to Ella, "Who's next?"

"What about the band members?"

"One at a time?"

"Yes, starting with the guitarist. He's the youngest."

Each of the band members provided a similar story. Johnny Toogood, the off-stage guitarist, told them that after he'd finished his cross-bow session in the archery gallery he went for a walk.

"In what direction?" asked Elsie.

"Out of the garden and towards the village. I suppose that's east? There's a bakery, a garage and a caravan park."

"Did you see or hear anything?"

"Not a thing to do with the well."

"Did anyone see you?"

"No, it was very quiet. Not much traffic on the road and not many people in the village. I came back for lunch and went back to my cross bow for about an hour in the afternoon. I only stopped when I heard the police siren. I walked across the gardens to see what all commotion was about."

Albert Hamm, the drummer, knew nothing, saw nothing and heard nothing. He'd been for a walk over the main road towards the sea.

"Nobody saw you?"

"Nope!"

Ronnie "Fingers" Ryan also knew nothing, saw nothing and heard nothing. "Someone said there was a church somewhere around here. I walked along Combpyne Lane for about a mile. I like churches, especially the church organs. But I couldn't find any church. I started feeling hungry so wandered back here. After lunch, I found a book about the Rousdon Estate. There was a church near the main house. I went in the wrong direction. They converted the church into a stunning house. I'd like to see that!"

Dave "Lazybones" Bartholomew, the double bassist, had intended to walk along a country lane to the west of Peek House. "I got about halfway along the lane when I felt tired, so I came back to the hotel, went up to my room and had a snooze. Almost missed dinner."

"And nobody saw you?"

"Well, no. This place is not like London. There's nobody around. It's deathly quiet."

"After dinner?"

"I carried on snoozing. This country lifestyle makes me feel so very tired."

When all band members had disappeared, Frank shrugged his shoulders. "If what they're saying is true, they all went for a walk, each in a different direction. Nobody saw them and they didn't see or hear anything either!"

"Who have we got left?" Elsie asked.

"Well, there's Emanuel the Spanish chef and Reeves. There's no other staff or guests around today."

All they could get out of Emanuel was that he had been in the kitchen all day since before breakfast.

"All I do is coo-ook, coo-ook, coo-ook!"

After Emanuel had left, Reeves confirmed that Emanuel had been in the kitchen every time he popped his head in.

"And where were you before lunch?" Frank asked Reeves.

"Preparing and serving our percolated coffee in the lounge, doing copious paperwork at the office desk in reception, readying the dining room for Sunday lunch, supervising the serving of said lunch."

"And after lunch?"

"Supervising the clearing away of another delightful meal, serving teas and home-made scones in the lounge although nobody partook of my availability and finally endeavouring to preserve the reputation of our lovely country hotel when your good selves..." he nodded towards Frank and Ella, "succeeded in summoning the attention of our local constabulary."

"And did anyone see you apart from your time in the dining room?"

"I sincerely hope not. A good butler aims to be silent and invisible until the moment he is required to assist the guests."

"Well, you're pretty good at that!" chortled Ella.

"Madame, I have had plenty of practice."

Elsie sat back in one of the comfortable leather club chairs in the lounge and tapped out a rapid beat on the rounded arms.

"I can't get a grip on this. No one has an alibi and yet no one strikes me as an obvious suspect."

"It's going to be another baffling case for Raleigh, Raleigh, Knowle and Hydon!"

"There is one clue." Elsie offered.

"What?"

"When they brought up the body, there was a card in her hand. Laminated to prevent it from getting smudged. As if someone wanted us to read it."

"And what did it say?"

Elsie consulted her notebook and read:

*"Ding, dong, bell,*
*Pussy's in the well.*
*Who put her in?*
*Little Johnny Flynn.*

*Best Wishes. Cornelius."*

"Johnny Flynn, who's he?"

"Cornelius' original drummer?"

"Could be."

"The original nursery rhyme had Johnny Flynn in its wording, didn't it?" replied Ella.

*"Ding, dong, bell,*
*Pussy's in the well.*
*Who put her in?*
*Little Johnny Flynn.*
*Who pulled her out?*
*Little Tommy Stout.*

*What a naughty boy was that*
*To try to drown poor pussy cat,*

*Who never did him any harm,*
*But ate all of the mice in the farmer's barn."*

Ella recited the whole nursery rhyme word perfectly.

"It's amazing what you remember from your childhood."

"It's an important clue, isn't it?" asked Frank.

"Or it could be a red herring!" replied Elsie, "To put us off the scent."

"Let's keep an open mind at the moment."

"Also, we've missed one person out," cut in Frank. "What about the lady we met at reception? She says she had just arrived. What if she'd already been here for some time?"

"Who is she?"

"Well, she signed her name in the register as Betty Brook-Spooner."

"Oh, my word, we've missed an obvious one there!"

"Spooner."

"I bet she's some kind of relation. She's come all the way down from deepest Northampton and taken revenge on Cornelius Spooner's wife. Perhaps for the money. Perhaps Diane mistreated her when they were young. Perhaps...."

"Perhaps, Ella, you would be so good as to fetch her down to the lounge. So, we can find out a few facts!"

Ella stopped her theorising and left the room.

"And we came here for a quiet break!" Frank mused.

Ella and Betty appeared in a few minutes. Elsie introduced Betty to the three of them and explained why she was here at the hotel.

"Hello, pleased to meet you. I'm Betty. Betty Brook-Spooner."

"Now, I'd like to know why you're at this particular

hotel?"

"I received a letter a few weeks ago telling me a room was booked in my name at the Cobb Country House Hotel in East Devon. The booking was for three days and the cost was a big fat zero. All I had to do was get here."

"I assume you came down by car?"

"No, I can't afford a car these days. I caught a National Express coach down to Victoria, then another one to Weymouth and then the X53 bus to Lyme Regis and onto here. It's much cheaper than by car or by rail. The bus dropped me just outside the gates. I had a little look around what there is of the village and then your lovely policemen let me through when I told them I was a guest."

"You received a letter," Frank revisited. "Who from?"

"I don't know. I phoned the hotel and the man in Reception told me that I was booked in on these dates. That was good enough for me."

Ella leaned forward, "Excuse me for being nosy but I happened to see you signed your name on the register as Betty Brook-Spooner."

"That's my name."

"Spooner. Any relation to Cornelius Spooner?"

"Of course. Once upon a time, I was married to him."

# CHAPTER 8

## WALK AWAY

"Another one!" said Ella.

"How many wives has he got?" asked Elsie.

"Two, I assume."

"So far!" replied Elsie.

Betty smiled at Elsie. "Is that all?"

"Yes, for now. Don't go anywhere without letting us know."

"Oh, I'm going to stick around. I love a good mystery." Betty rose from her chair and left the room.

Frank stood up and walked over to the window. "There's so much to think about. I didn't really envisage us becoming involved in another murder investigation."

"Could she have just fallen down the well?"

"Yes. The fall certainly killed her," said Elsie. "But we don't know yet if she was pushed? If she was, then that points to murder."

"We heard a short scream but thinking about it, that may have been cut off by the fall."

"So, the scream was the last thing she did…" Ella stopped. "This is too awful. Frank, tomorrow morning, can we get away from here - just for a while? Clear our heads and come back recharged?"

"A walk?"

"Absolutely."

"Do you have one in mind or do you want me to choose?"

"You choose."

"Well, I found a website with lots of walks around Lyme Regis. The University of the Third Age. They've got a series of walks sourced by a lovely old lady called Liz Jones. She was part of the U3A walking group."

"U3A?" asked Elsie.

"University of the Third Age! Weren't you listening?" cried Ella. "Sorry, shouldn't have raised my voice!"

"You two go and have your walk. I've been called back to Exeter to report to Inspector Wilkins about this case. I'll see you tomorrow probably. We might know more about how she died, then." Elsie stood up and gathered her notebook and hat. "Could I suggest that you stay here for a few extra days? I'd appreciate your input as we sort this out. Shouldn't take too long."

"I was going to suggest the same thing," agreed Frank. "I think Kennaway Coopers can survive without us for a while longer!"

The next morning Frank and Ella were the only ones in the dining room for breakfast. Martha served them.

"How's your sister?"

"So excited to be part of such an adventure!"

"Oh, to be young and innocent!"

Reeves was not on duty yet, it seemed. After a simple meal of cereal and toast, Frank and Ella, put on their walking boots and gear and headed off in their car past the policeman at the gate, through Rousdon along the A3052, and down into the ancient Domesday town of Lyme Regis. At the bottom of Broad Street, they were lucky to find an empty parking space in the Cobb Gate car park.

"We're going to make our way to Uplyme and then round in a circle back to here," Frank informed Ella as they stood by the car park looking out over Lyme Bay.

The water was calm. They could see across to the Cobb where several tourists appeared to be enacting scenes from John Fowles' *The French Lieutenants Woman* - the women staring mysteriously out to sea.

"Did you know the book was set in the town and the film was shot here?"

"Actually yes. But do you know who played the lead female role?"

"Easy. Mama Mia's Meryl Streep."

Frank was, as usual, well prepared. He had already downloaded the coming excursion onto his phone. He had honed up on some snippets of factual information to enhance his enjoyment of the walk.

"It's a reasonably easy walk, there's a couple of short hills, it's about 5 miles in length. We'll easily finish before dinner."

They turned their back on the sea and made their way across the road, through the Broad Street carpark and over the footbridge to Town Mill. Frank and Ella spent a short while looking at the ancient, restored watermill and its flour mill, café and craft studios before following the

Riverside Walk beside the River Lim before emerging eventually at Windsor Terrace. From there, they followed the path with the swiftly flowing narrow river on their left and imposing houses raised above them on their right. Leaving the path behind them and heading across a field, they passed what looked like an old mill and a secluded cottage before emerging on a road. The road sign read Mill Lane. At the end, they found a leafy footpath opposite. The map called it The Glen. This eventually led to a relatively busy thoroughfare - the main road that led from Lyme Regis into Uplyme.

"That was very pleasant," commented Frank. "Not too strenuous."

Ella popped into the petrol station shop to buy a drink and some confectionery before joining Frank by the cricket pitch and tennis courts. Here they stopped and enjoyed a short break watching some children playing cricket. Alongside the open space of the cricket ground, the Uplyme Village Hall looked modern and well maintained. The sun was shining, and all was well with the world.

"Isn't it amazing how a gentle walk restores the soul?" remarked Ella.

"Yeah, clears out the refuse and clarifies your thinking."

"Are you talking about Diane's death?"

"Yes, I thought at first it was a horrible accident, but Elsie comments convinced me that we've got another murder on our hands."

"So, who are our suspects?" murmured Ella.

"Well, in no order of guilt, I'd say Cornelius, the four band members especially Albert the drummer, Betty the wife, Emanuel the chef, Reeves the butler and Mary the waitress. I'm not including you and I on our list!"

"I should think not. There's no other guests, are there?"

"No. And I've not seen any other members of staff."

"But forget that woman we saw by the bins."

"Of course, Annie Saxon, Cornelius' Number One Fan."

"Yes, there was something not quite right about her."

Suddenly a cricket ball landed with a thump nearby.

"Oi, mister, can we have our ball back?"

Frank got slowly to his feet and picked up the cricket ball. "Here you are." He threw it back on the full straight into the wicketkeeper's gloves.

"Good throw, sir. Thanks!"

Frank smiled and waved a hand in recognition. "Shall we get going again?" He offered the same hand to Ella. She used it to leap to her feet.

"Let's hit the road, Jack."

They crossed the playing field keeping to the right-hand side away from the youngster's cricket match and found the footpath across the fields. It was signed the East Devon Way.

"I've seen a couple of those signs now," said Frank. "Lyme Regis is in Dorset."

"But it's right on the border. I think we're back in Sunny Devon."

"The East Devon Way runs from Lyme Regis to Exmouth. That's almost 40 miles."

"It runs quite near to Otterbury."

"Yes, if we carried on this footpath, we could walk most of the way home!"

"Not today. Let's just follow your map route back to Lyme Regis."

The footpath crossed a large grassy field before it came out onto a lovely lane with a tall hedge on one side and bungalows on the other. They continued straight ahead to join, according to their map, Cannington Lane. The narrow tarmacked lane was engulfed in hedges and fern greenery on both sides and devoid of many bends. They would be able to see any motor traffic a long time before it reached them. However, none appeared. They walked onwards, climbing steadily, the tranquility only interrupted by the ever-present chatter of birds until after Cannington Farm, they espied a railway viaduct.

"I didn't know Lyme Regis had a railway station," observed Ella.

"Not anymore. I've read about this viaduct. It's called the Cannington Viaduct. It was built in 1901."

"I can see ten arches, but look, on the right, one of the arches has been split in two. It looks like two church windows, one on top of the other!"

"That's because one of those pillars sank a bit after construction. There was a stream running through it. They had built an extra bit of support to stop it falling down!"

"What's it made of? Looks like cement."

"Most of it is. They brought the cement by sea into the Cobb Harbour at Lyme Regis and got it up here via a cableway."

"Wow! I'd like to have seen that! So where did the trains go to from here?"

"Axminster Junction. The branch line opened in 1903 but they'd had a difficult time building through all these hills and valleys. There was just one station, Combpyne, between Axminster and Lyme Regis but loads of steep curves and challenging gradients."

"Where's Combpyne?"

"To the west of here. We're actually not too far from the

Cobb Country House hotel."

"This was built way before British Rail?"

"Yes, the London and South Western Railway built it. The line operated from 1903 to 1963. Passenger numbers dwindled. Then, in 1963, they closed the line, like loads of others…"

"Let me guess, Doctor Beeching?"

"Spot on. What a tourist attraction it would have been these days if they'd kept it running."

"How do you know all this info?"

"I did some reading up last night. I always like to be prepared!"

They had passed under the viaduct and turned sharp left onto a field footpath running parallel up to the viaduct. At the top of the field, they followed some markers alongside a house before following the road that led from the house. Just past the next set of houses they turned right onto a footpath and climbed through some woods before coming out onto Gore Lane. Turning right again, they followed the road as it led them to Ware Cross. Frank and Ella continued leisurely over the crossroads and walked along a lovely hedge-lined narrow road until they reached a footpath marked also as a private drive.

"Are we allowed to go through here?" queried Ella.

"The map and the directions both say go this way. It leads to the South West Coast Path."

They reached the Coast Path and with views of Lyme Bay glistening in the midday sun, they trudged their way down into Lyme Regis.

"Look out for fossils!"

"Not up here. They'll be down at the foot of the cliffs."

"We are *not* going to be scrambling around there. Looks very unsafe to me."

"You may have a point. We're always hearing about cliff falls, all the way along the Jurassic Coast."

"Perhaps we'll save the fossil hunting till another day."

"Another day? Never."

"A trivia question for you, Ella. Which famous authority on fossils was born in Lyme Regis?"

"You always love to throw out these obscure questions. That's the result of spending most of your life as a teacher!"

"That's as may be, but do you know? Frank asked again.

"He or she?"

"She."

"Well, that has to be Mary... Anning." Ella had read about this eminent expert on dinosaur skeletons but because she was a woman, they wouldn't admit her to the Geological Society of London.

Frank nodded. "Even though she knew far more than most of the old fossils there!!"

The Coast Path brought them out above the Cobb. The harbour was still dotted with tourists. Immediately below them, the car park was filling up with visitors. Frank and Ella walked contentedly, hand in hand, through the crowds of tourists, along the sunny promenade. Children were playing on the sands and in the sea. Ahead of them loomed the highest point in Dorset, Golden Cap.

"One day I'd like to climb that," said Ella enthusiastically.

"We just have to follow the Coast Path. It goes up there and on to West Bay."

"For now, let's just go back to the car."

They arrived back at the Cobb Country House Hotel a

little late for dinner, but Chef Emanuel had kept something back for them. They thanked him with the aid of expressive hands signals. He smiled and nodded as if he understood. Frank and Ella went to sit in the dining room by the windows that looked out onto the lush garden.

They enjoyed their meal. Martha, Mary's elder sister, popped in now and again to make sure they had everything they needed.

"No-one would have guessed what happened here yesterday. It's a charming English country house full of charming guests and staff dedicated to fulfilling all our needs!"

"Hmm, that's a bit over the top."

"I know, but you know what I mean."

"Let's take our coffee out into the gardens."

They whiled away the afternoon, a very subdued Cornelius came and sat with them for a while. Frank and Ella shared details of their morning walk around Lyme Regis with him. After Cornelius had wandered away, Frank and Ella spied Betty sitting on her own, apparently reading a book.

A little later, they could see that Cornelius went and sat with her. They appeared to be enjoying a friendly conversation conducted at an acceptable volume.

"No arguments there," pointed out Ella. "They appear very relaxed in each other's company."

Reeves appeared and offered them an afternoon cup of tea and a slice of fruit cake. They accepted eagerly. He moved on to Cornelius and Betty and repeated the offer. They also accepted. A joke and a chuckle rose from Cornelius' lips. Betty smiled and reached out to touch his hand. Reeves discreetly withdrew.

Ella hummed a melody and quietly sang some lyrics she remembered from her childhood:

*How many kinds of sweet flowers grow*
*In an English country garden?*
*We'll tell you now of some that we know*
*Those we miss you'll surely pardon  ...*

# CHAPTER 9

# DROWNING IN THE SEA OF LOVE

Frank and Ella tore themselves away from the garden to prepare for their evening meal. As they walked past Reception a fashionably dressed female guest was waiting for someone to come and serve her.

"Hello," said Ella as they passed, "Can I help?"

"I'm waiting for someone to sign me in and show me to my room. It's a lovely building but the customer service is a tad disastrous!"

"Have you rung the bell?"

"Yes. No response!"

"Well, it's been a strange last couple of days."

As Ella spoke, Reeves appeared out of nowhere.

"Good afternoon, madame, may I be of assistance?"

"Yes, you may. I'm booked in for a couple of days. Where do I sign in?"

"Please wait one moment, madame, whilst I retrieve the register." He reached under the reception counter and brought out a brown leather-bound book. "Please put your name and address here." Reeves pointed to the next space on the page.

"Cor, that's strange."

"Pardon, madame?"

"Well, you've got a Cornelius Spooner staying here."

"Yes, madame." Reeves did not seem too impressed.

"And Betty Spooner. I haven't seen her for years. Not since…. Well, not for a long while."

"Please sign here and here, Mrs…"

Reeves subtly looked at her entry. "…. Jane Spooner."

Frank and Ella looked at each other. Eyebrows were raised.

Back in their room, Ella sat on the bed and puffed out her cheeks.

"Well, well, well! This is getting very interesting."

"Has Cornelius lured them here?"

"He did seem very friendly with Betty."

"Yes."

Ella frowned. "On the other hand, are they all out to get Cornelius?"

"Or, are we just reading too much into it? Was Diane really murdered? Was it an accident?"

Frank nodded. "Whatever happened, it doesn't make any sense at the moment. What's going on?"

"Coincidence?"

Frank tapped something into his smart phone.

"A coincidence will always be a coincidence until its significance is realized," he read.

"Very profound."

"And hopefully true!"

"What do we do next?"

"Get ready for our evening meal. After our walk today, I'm starving."

Everybody filed into the dining room the minute the gong was struck by Reeves. Everything had been re-arranged so there was one big table stretching half the length of the room.

"I took the liberty of putting all our guests together."

"Safety in numbers," chortled Johnny the guitarist.

Reeves almost smiled. "Yes, sir, I had that in mind."

Being together on one table enabled the steady flow of conversation. Cornelius sat in the middle of one side facing the outside windows. Betty and Jane sat either side of him. Frank and Ella sat opposite Cornelius with Albert and Davy, the drummer and double bassist on their left at the end of the table and Johnny Toogood and Ronnie, the guitarist and pianist on the right-hand side end.

"This is Betty," Cornelius introduced waving his hand in Betty's direction. "She's my second wife."

Betty smiled at everyone gathered around the table.

"This lady is Jane, my third wife. I realise now that I have been blessed with good women throughout my life."

"It's a pity, you didn't recognise it at the time!" replied Jane.

"And is it true," asked Johnny, "that the lady in the well was your first wife?"

"Yes, it is," answered Cornelius. His fallen face immediately betrayed his immense anguish. "It was a sad, sad accident, I'm told."

There was a murmuring from some parts of the table, but no one offered any alternative opinion.

The meal continued with Martha and Reeves waiting upon the assembled throng.

"Well, what are going to do this evening?" asked Albert the drummer.

"No practice tonight," replied Cornelius, "I'm not in the mood."

"What about a walk into Lyme Regis?" offered Ronnie the pianist.

"That's miles away," moaned Cornelius.

"If sir would allow me to make a suggestion?" Reeves interrupted.

"Go on, Mr. Butler."

"At the hotel, we have a mini-bus that we use to transport guests to the railway station. I would be delighted to ferry you down to the town and pick you up later in the evening."

Smiles emerged all along the table.

"Excellent idea," beamed Johnny the guitarist. "Is the sea warm enough to swim in?"

"I believe so, sir."

"Well then, I'm taking my trunks!"

Jane Spooner turned up her nose. "You won't catch me dipping my toes in the water."

"Oh, come on. It'll be fun. A little doggy paddle and a splash around will do us all the world of good."

Betty leaned forward to talk to Jane. "I agree with you. Too cold by far."

Cornelius turned to her. "I'd be very surprised to see you swimming! When we were married, you didn't even know how to swim. Has that changed?"

Betty bowed her head and nodded.

"Don't matter," Albert continued, "plenty of other things to do. A walk on the Cobb, an ice cream on the prom. You could sit on one of the benches and just watch the world go by."

Everyone cheered up at the thought of getting away from the hotel for a couple of hours. The meal was concluded in a jovial manner.

"We'll meet outside reception in twenty minutes," boomed Cornelius.

Everyone got up from the table and vacated the dining room.

Frank and Ella were the only ones who remained.

"You don't fancy another walk, do you?" muttered Frank.

"No, we're on holiday. Let's just go into the guest lounge and stare at some meaningless drivel on the television!"

Frank smiled, nodded and took Ella's hand.

"Yes, me lady," he responded in his best Parker impersonation.

There were twenty-five minutes of excited chatter, slamming of doors and footsteps rushing up and down stairs before the mini-bus took its occupants down to Lyme Regis and peace was restored. Frank and Ella took their iPads into the guest room and enjoyed an evening of American police procedures, British soaps and a strange, subtitled film from Czechoslovakia that neither one of them understood. The plot made no sense, the photography was atmospheric, and the misty forest scenery was pleasant on the eyes.

*Now, where is she? She said she was heading for the Cobb.*

*Wait a minute, there she is.*

*It's just like that film with Sheryl whatshername.*

*Oh, this is going to be too easy. Just stay there, little lady.*

*Just stay by the edge.*

*Yes, have a look down and see how deep it is.*

*Right, concentrate.*

*Gloves on?*

*Mallet at the ready?*

*Calling card at the ready?*

*Don't worry, little lady.*

*Don't you just love how unquestioning they are?*

*You won't feel a thing. Well, not much anyway.*

*One knock on the head, one little push and the deed is done.*

*Sweet dreams.*

*Drum roll, please.*

Frank and Ella were just dozing off when the phone rang in the reception area. It startled Ella, but Frank said, "Don't worry. Someone'll get it in a minute."

The phone carried on ringing.

"Where's Reeves?"

"Didn't he go into Lyme Regis with everybody else?"

"There must be someone on duty?"

"I'll go and..." The phone stopped ringing and both Ella and Frank could hear the baffled tones of Emanuel, the Hotel Chef. He spoke slowly in very broken English.

"I think he needs some help," smiled Frank.

Ella got up and went into the reception area. Emanuel held out the phone to her and vigorously shrugged his shoulders.

"Hello, can I help you?"

"Yeah, hi, it's Johnny, Johnny Toogood. Is that Ella or Betty?"

"It's Ella. Is everything OK?"

"Well maybe. And maybe not. You see, we can't find Betty or Cornelius. We were hoping they'd caught a bus or a taxi back to the hotel."

"I don't think they're here. We would have heard them."

Frank had overheard most of the conversation. "What room are they in?" he whispered.

Ella shrugged her shoulders. "Check the register."

"Hold on," announced Johnny, "Panic over. Here comes Cornelius. Typical, he's in his own little world."

"Right, good. Is Betty with him?"

"No. I don't think so. I'm gonna put you on mute whilst I check."

The phone went quiet. Frank found the register under the counter and soon located Betty's name.

"She signed in just before we were going to start questioning Mary. The Somers Room."

"I remember," said Ella. "I took her up there."

The phone crackled back into life. "Hi, can you hear me?"

"Yes, loud and clear."

"We've got Cornelius but still no sign of Betty."

"I've found her room number. I'll go and check."

Ella handed Frank the phone and set off up the stairs.

"Hi, Johnny," announced Frank. "We're just checking for you now. Is anybody else missing?"

"No, we're all here, except Betty. We're all standing by the minibus. Reeves is waiting to drive us back to the hotel. But we can't leave Betty behind. Cornelius is getting a bit distraught. Think's something might have happened to her. I do hope she's…"

"Which car park are you in?"

"The Holmbush on the Sidmouth Road. It's quite a hike back up from the Cobb, I can tell you."

Ella came rushing back down the stairs shaking her head. She grabbed the phone.

"She's not in her room. I knocked and shouted but there's no reply."

"Oh, my word, it's going to make Corn…" groaned Johnny.

His next words were drowned out by a loud siren-like noise.

"What was that?" asked Ella.

"An ambulance. It's just turned the corner by the car park. It's heading down to the Cobb."

Frank and Ella looked at each other.

"Look, Johnny. Start searching for her. Why doesn't Reeves stay by the minibus and the rest of you go searching? Give us a call when you find her."

"Yeah, good idea. Speak to you soon."

The call was ended, and Ella put the phone back on its cradle.

"Frank, I've got a very bad feeling about this."

"You and me both," he nodded.

Two hours later, the minibus drove into the car park and a weary bunch of guests straggled through reception.

"Any sign of her?" asked Albert Hamm.

"She's not with you?"

"No, we waited and waited. Cornelius phoned the police and spoke to that tall PC who came here when…"

"PC Hydon. What did he say?"

"Told us to get back along. Which we translated to mean go back to the hotel. So here we are."

Frank went to the kitchen to tell Emanuel the party had returned. Emanuel warmed up some hot chocolate he had prepared an hour ago.

"Why did she just go off on her own?" Cornelius wheezed. He looked drained and defeated. "We all started off together but some of us walk quicker than others and we…"

"Yes, but I would have slowed down," said Johnny.

"She was walking quicker than you!"

"Well, I would have sped up. Oh, I know what I mean. It's such a mess. First Diane, and now Betty."

"What do you mean? She's not dead, she's just lost. She probably met up with someone. I expect she'll find somewhere to stay for the night."

"She's not that sort of woman. She's a lady." Cornelius was shocked.

"Far too good for you," chuckled Albert Hamm.

Cornelius stared daggers at Albert the drummer.

"Drinks anyone?"

Ella offered the hot chocolate around to everyone who wanted some. Most took a few sips and then wandered off to bed. It was late, too late for an inquisition.

Reeves locked up and silence once more descended upon the Cobb Country House Hotel.

It was a restless night. Ella kept expecting to hear the front doorbell being rung and a bedraggled Betty marching in. But no such event occurred. Everyone appeared at breakfast in a sombre mood. Cornelius looked even worse than last night.

"Sleep well?" asked Johnny.

"Not a wink. Kept replaying the evening. When did I miss her? What should I have done?"

"Don't worry. She'll be back. I expect she'll…"

The front doorbell rang. Everyone looked at each other. Cornelius breathed a sigh of relief.

"That'll be her now. I hope she's all right."

Reeves had disappeared, presumably to let Betty in.

The dining room door opened.

All eyes turned towards the door in expectation. In walked Sergeant Elsie Knowle.

"Where's Betty?" cried Cornelius. There was fear in his eyes. Elsie stood there shifting from foot to foot.

"Where is she?" repeated Cornelius.

"It's my unpleasant duty to inform you that there's been a terrible accident. Betty Brook-Spooner was pulled out of the sea last night. She slipped and fell off the Cobb."

"Is she OK? Is she in hospital?"

"No, I'm afraid, she's not OK." Elsie Knowle did not like being the centre of attention when she had such awful news to impart. "No, she's dead."

# CHAPTER 10

# ANNIE'S SONG

Cornelius's face turned a whiter shade of pale.

"What do you mean she's dead?" he stammered.

Sergeant Knowle still moved from one foot to the other. This was the most unpleasant part of her job.

"Well sir," she replied, "we retrieved a body from the water by the Cobb. Following on from your conversation with PC Hydon, we've concluded, that the body is Betty Brook-Spooner. We'll need somebody to come down to the hospital to identify her but there's little doubt, I'm afraid."

"How do you mean - little doubt?"

"Simply because we found a handbag on the Cobb close by where she fell in. When we checked the contents, we found her name on a couple of the items."

Everyone was stunned. There was not a sound in the room. After a couple of minutes, Cornelius stood up.

"I'll do it," he muttered. "If someone gives me a lift down to the hospital, I'll identify her."

"Thank you, Sir," said Sergeant Knowle. "PC Hydon will

take you down to the hospital whenever you're ready."

Johnny stood up as well. He dropped his serviette onto his half-eaten meal. "I assume that's the end of breakfast!"

Everybody else put down their knives, forks and cups of tea and made as if to leave as well.

"Excuse me. Please wait a moment. I'd prefer you not to leave the premises until further notice."

Everyone in the room turned towards Sergeant Knowle.

"Does that mean that you think her death might be suspicious?" asked Ella.

"We're keeping an open mind - at the moment."

Reeves the Butler ceremoniously raised a hand and asked for silence. "Ladies and gentlemen, on behalf of Cobb Country House Hotel, I would ask you to keep this little incident to ourselves. I am sure the police will soon conclude that it was an unfortunate accident. Until then, there is no reason for anybody outside of this room to be informed. Thank you."

And with that, he walked serenely out of the room.

Albert, the drummer, turned to Ronnie "Fingers" Ryan and in a voice loud enough for anyone to hear said "it's like being in a totalitarian country. We are not free to say anything here. Keep quiet. Don't snitch. Could be you next?"

As Ella was moving towards the door, she whispered to Frank "Is he being serious?"

Frank shrugged and followed Ella out of the dining room and back to their bedroom.

Ella sat in the chair by the window and looked out at the glorious, morning sky.

"Do you think it was an accident? Did she jump or was she pushed?"

Frank stood by her, one hand on his shoulder. "I don't really know. If it was an accident, then it's a tragedy. If she was pushed, then it's murder."

"And Cornelius?" sighed Ella, "he was the last one back to the minibus. Could he have pushed her?"

"Why would he?"

"Perhaps she had some information that he didn't want to be made public?"

"Perhaps. Or maybe it's another one of those coincidences. And I'm not sure I believe in coincidences anymore."

They sat there in silence, both staring out of the window. The gardens, as much as they could see of them, bloomed golden in the morning sun. The sky was completely blue. The weather outside seemed totally out of kilter with the mood within the hotel.

"What are we going to do today?"

"Well, I'd like to talk to everybody who was in that minibus yesterday evening. I would like to find out where they were and who they were with. I'd like to hear each of their alibis."

Ella was still looking out of the window. "Frank, look over there on the other side of the driveway. Isn't that Annie Saxon? The woman we saw by the dustbins?"

"Yes, what's she doing here?"

Ella turned to him with a look of intent. "Why don't we go and ask her?"

Annie was still sitting on the other side of the driveway when Frank and Ella approached her. She had a rucksack on her back and her knitted woollen hat in her hand.

"Hello, fancy seeing you again. Are you looking for Cornelius?"

Annie seemed in a trance.

"Oh, hello, you two. No, I'm just... I don't really know what I'm doing here."

"Are you okay?" asked Ella.

"Yes, I suppose so. I heard about Betty. Well, at least, I mean... I saw what happened. I was there when they pulled her body from the water. It was horrible. Later, I heard the policeman saying who it was. He said, Spooner. I thought there might be a connection with Cornelius. There is a connection, isn't there?"

Frank nodded. "Maybe."

"What's happening?"

Ella sat down alongside her and put an arm around her shoulder.

"It's all been quite horrible," said Ella.

They found a quiet place in the garden. Ella helped Annie off with her rucksack. She found a flask in there and poured Annie a drink. It was piping hot tea.

"Here. Drink this."

Annie sipped regularly. Ella noticed the glimmer of life trickle into her eyes.

"Are you feeling better?"

Annie nodded.

"Then perhaps you'd like to tell us why you're here."

"You know why I'm here. I'm following Cornelius around the country. I've seen all of his concerts on this tour. I haven't missed a concert for over 10 years."

"So, you must know a lot about him?" Frank asked.

"Yes, of course. I'm his number one fan. You ask me any question about Cornelius and the Portobello Crooners, and I'll give you the answer."

"Well for a start," Ella mused, "How many wives has he got?"

Annie laughed. "That's easy. Cornelius is on wife number six."

"Six!" Frank shook his head in wonder. "and we've already met three of them."

"And out of those three, two are dead!" said Ella.

Annie's face betrayed a look of horror. "I know. Is somebody protecting Jane? And what about the other three? Has somebody contacted them? Are they still alive?"

"I don't know the answers to any of those questions," said Ella. "We'll need to speak to Sergeant Knowle about that. I'm interested in his wives."

"Yes," agreed Frank. "He seemed to be on good terms with the three we've met so far. Was that true or was it just an act?"

"He is now. Back in the day, he had a wandering eye. That's what it was like in the sixties. He was always on the road playing concerts or in the studio recording songs. He didn't have a settled life. He moved from one place to the other. It was the same with his women. He moved from one to the other. None of them liked it. They tried to tie him down by marrying him. Apart from the first one, they had to get him divorced before they could marry him. It must have cost him a fortune paying maintenance. He was a big spender. All the pop stars were. In the sixties. He was young and they just threw money at him for a few years. So, he spent it. None of his managers encouraged him to save any. That's why he's still touring today. He needs the money."

"You say he is on good terms with his wives now. Were there ever any occasions when he treated them badly enough for any of them to want to kill him? And conversely, did any of his wives treat *him* so badly but he would want to kill *them*?"

"No, he isn't that sort of person. They all loved him and he, in return, in his way, loved them. But he's a wanderer, a vagabond, a rolling stone. He can't stay too long in any one place and he didn't use to be able to stay with any one person."

"That would explain the attitudes of the three wives. They wouldn't hear a bad word against him. They understood his ways. They didn't like it. But they understood." Ella was pleased with her summary.

"Yes, that's true. You've hit the nail right on the head." Anne nodded. She went on speaking enthusiastically now. "He's a lovely man. No, more than that. He's gorgeous. Talented. Charming. Handsome." She smiled to herself.

"What about his bands? Asked Frank.

"Well, he always had a drummer, a pianist and a double bassist. Right from the early days, it was a stand-up double bass. They used to swivel it around on its spike. Cornelius used to chase the instrument around in circles waiting for a laugh from the audience. It always worked. He always got one."

"No guitarist then?"

"No, he took care of the guitar. Electric. National Studio 66 when he first made the grade. Then he switched to a Rickenbacker like George Harrison. Then he played a Stratocaster. And after that, he was always switching guitars. Like his band. He never kept the same band for any time. In the early days, he must have changed group members at least every tour. Sometimes he changed the band two or three times during a tour. There are so many former Portobello Crooners that even I can't recall them all."

"What about this version of the band?"

"Now this is where it becomes interesting. He's kept this band together now for over four years. Except for Johnny Toogood. He only joined last year. That's simply because Cornelius is developing arthritis in his fingers. He can't play the guitar anymore."

"I thought he was faking it the other night," interrupted Frank.

"You were right. Johnny Toogood is the best guitarist he's ever had. He's young but he's very shy on-stage. But Cornelius was happy for Johnny to play off-stage and almost out of sight. Cornelius makes it appear that nothing's changed. In fact, Johnny makes Cornelius sound better than he's ever sounded."

"I'd agree with that!" Frank had enjoyed Johnny Toogood's playing far more than he had expected.

"And what's more, Johnny is happier to play the invisible man role. He has a moan now and then but when Cornelius offers him a spot on stage, he always turns him down."

"How do you know that?" asked Ella.

"Albert Hamm told me. In fact, he's told me that several times. Albert and I are good friends. Have been since before he joined the Crooners."

"Do any of the Portobello Crooners have a gripe with Cornelius?" asked Ella.

"Of course. What band doesn't have a gripe with a band leader who dictates what they play, how they play, where they play and when they play? But that doesn't mean they would kill his wives."

"Do you think someone is deliberately killing Cornelius' wives to get at Cornelius?"

"I don't know the answer to that. They could be. It could also just be a horrendous coincidence. Accidents. These things happen."

Ella nodded in sympathy. She didn't notice Frank's subtle shake of his head.

Annie sat there staring into her flask cup.

Frank decided to go on the offensive. "You said you were there when the body was found?"

"Yes."

"Where were you before the body was found?"

"I was in Lyme Regis enjoying the evening crowds."

"Were you near the Cobb?"

"Of course, I was. Along with several thousand other people. None of them laid a finger on poor Betty and neither did I."

"Did you see any people that you recognised from the band or from the hotel?"

"No. There were so many people wandering around. It's been pretty crowded in Lyme Regis all week."

Reeves appeared at Ella's shoulder and delicately coughed. "Ladies and gentleman, I thought it prudent to announce that morning coffee is being served in the lounge."

"Thank you, we'll be there in a while," Ella replied but Reeves had already turned his back and was walking towards the maze to announce this information to another group.

Annie stared after him before turning towards Frank. She reached out a hand towards him and tapped him on the sleeve. "I saw that man in Lyme Regis last night."

"That's Reeves, the hotel's butler. He drove everyone down to Lyme Regis in the hotel minibus," said Ella.

"I'm sure he did. But I saw him with Betty last night."

# CHAPTER 11

# HENERY THE EIGHTH,
# I AM, I AM

Frank and Ella could get nothing more out of Annie. "I only glimpsed them together for a minute before I lost them in the crowd."

"Were they arguing?"

"I was too far away to tell. Look, you're missing your morning coffee. I need to get back to my guest house for lunch. There's a bus due in 10 minutes, so I'll leave you be. Thanks for the chat. I enjoyed trawling through the memories."

Annie got up, gathered her rucksack and threw the remains of the tea from her flask into the shrubbery. She then made off determinedly towards the drive.

Ella stood and waved goodbye and then caught up with Frank who was already heading in for his morning cup of tea.

"I liked her," said Ella.

"I could tell. She had some interesting points to make,

and she made them very convincingly."

"Was she telling the truth about Cornelius?" pondered Ella.

"Sometimes people see the world through rose tinted glasses."

"Meaning?"

"She's in love with Cornelius and would defend him to the very last - in spite of any evidence to the contrary."

"You're telling me to keep an open mind, aren't you?"

"You read me like the proverbial book!"

Morning coffee was a sedate affair. There were only a few people gathered in the lounge.

"No Cornelius?" Ella asked Jane.

"I haven't seen him since breakfast."

Albert the drummer was the only member of the band in the room. "Think he went out for a walk. Probably needs to clear his head. These last few days have been a bit of a shock for him."

"We've been talking to Annie, Annie Saxon. She says she knew you from before you joined the band."

"Yeah, that's right. She got me the gig. Previous drummer could hardly keep time, especially after a heavy night on the booze. I'd played in a support band and we struck up a friendship, if you know what I mean, after a couple of the gigs. She recommended me to Cornelius and the rest is history."

Ella smiled and whispered to Frank. "Well, that bit was true."

The rest of the conversation meandered inconsequentially, and the little group split up and went their separate ways. Frank was looking out of the window and saw Elsie Knowle, dressed in her civilian clothes, stepping out of her own car and then heading towards the hotel entrance.

Frank and Ella met her at the lounge door. "Fancy a bit of food and a chat?" Elsie asked, "It's a lovely day."

"Sure," said Frank, "Any developments?"

"Not here," replied Elsie.

Frank and Ella popped to their room to grab their coats and some money. They climbed into Elsie's car and were soon driving towards Lyme Regis on the A3052. As they cruised down the hill into the town, Elsie signalled right at the Holmbush car park and they sauntered down the steep hill of Cobb Road leading to the harbour. The beach car park was only about half full as Elsie paid for her car park ticket.

"I thought we'd try The Cobb Arms. It's normally quite crowded at lunchtimes but it has its fair share of nooks and crannies and quiet corners. We can talk without being disturbed."

"Where's Alf?"

"Playing with his gadgets. He's gone on a crowd control refresher course so he can use his wi-fi whistle."

"How does it work?" asked Frank.

"I've yet to meet anybody who can answer that question." Elsie shrugged her shoulders and headed off rapidly towards the Cobb Arms.

Frank and Ella followed behind and soon they were ensconced in a quiet corner. "I've booked a table for four," commented Elsie as they ordered meals off the fish menu and drinks from the bar. Soon they were seated at a corner table separated from any others by a wooden partition.

"You said four? Do we need room to expand?" Frank put his coat onto the spare chair.

"All in good time," Elsie said with a conspiratorial smile.

The drinks arrived from the bar. "Food'll be about twenty minutes," said the young waitress.

"No hurry."

"All I seem to do these past few days is eat and drink," admitted Ella.

"You're feeding the mind and watering the soul," exclaimed Frank.

"And now you're helping me to solve two murders," added Elsie.

She took a sip of her drink and sighed with some contentment.

"Are you going to get us up to date with any developments?" asked Frank.

"Yes. I wondered how long it would take you to ask!" She smiled as she took out her notebook.

"First of all, let me tell you about two strange but perhaps vital clues. These convince me that we *are* investigating two murders. In amongst the clothes of Diane Streamer and in Betty's handbag, we found two cards. They were postcard size. Each had a typewritten verse."

Elsie stopped to take another sip of her drink.

"Go on," urged Ella.

"Diane's verse was…" Elsie consulted her notebook and read:

*"Ding, dong, bell,*
*Pussy's in the well.*
*Who put her in?*
*Little Johnny Flynn.*
*Who pulled her out?*
*Little Tommy Stout.*
*What a naughty boy was that*
*To try to drown poor pussy cat,*

*Who never did him any harm,*
*But ate all of the mice in the farmer's barn."*

"You told us about that back at the hotel. It's the old nursery rhyme," burst out Ella.

"Correct. I presume the murderer was trying to tell us that Diane was deliberately pushed down the well."

"Premeditated," offered Frank.

"And was Betty's also a nursery rhyme?"

"Almost but not quite. It was a quote from a Beatles song." Elsie gave them time to think.

"Octopus' Garden?" speculated Frank. Ella tapped him on the arm and quoted:

*"I'd like to be under the sea,*
*In an octopus's garden in the shade*
*He'd let us in, knows where we've been*
*In his octopus's garden in the shade."*

"Spot on," Elsie laughed. "I thought Frank would get it, not you!"

"We both love the Beatles, not just Frank!"

"Again, premeditated?" said Frank.

"This is crazy. Both deaths were made to look like accidents. They both appeared to have slipped and fell-one into a well, one into the sea. Why would someone advertise the fact that their deaths are premeditated murders?"

"I didn't share this with you back at the hotel. The most interesting part is if you turn the card over."

Frank did and looked shocked.

"What is it?" asked Ella.

"It's writing. It says *'Best Wishes. Cornelius.'*" Frank thought for a moment. "What I find most interesting," he continued, "is that full stop. Not a comma, but a full stop."

"You and your punctuation. Once a schoolteacher, always a schoolteacher."

"I think it has significance."

"Cornelius is killing his first two wives? Can't be?"

"Either Cornelius is guilty of these two murders or this is the work of a very warped mind," admitted Elsie.

"Why would he make it so obvious? Or has this all been meticulously planned to point the finger at him?"

"Weren't both wives just invited down here?" asked Ella.

"Yes, who did that? Another twist."

"What about the third wife - Jane Spooner?"

"Is she out for revenge or is she a potential victim?" Frank mused.

"Oh no, not another victim. We're veering into Midsomer Murder territory. But in this case, it's not funny."

Elsie held a hand up. "Hold on for a moment, we're straying away into conjecture. Let's get back on task. We have two deaths and two apparent clues in the form of two verses."

Their dinners arrived at that opportune moment and all three spent a few minutes enjoying their own particular choices of meal.

Frank took up the reins again. "Forget about the signature. What can we learn from those two clues? Somebody with a musical knowledge that stretches back to the Beatles. Someone old enough to remember their nursery rhymes. That could be any of our suspects."

"Talking of suspects," continued Ella, "which of our guests are under suspicion?"

Elsie finished a mouthful and then once more consulted her notebook. "Well, I'd include all the members of the band. That's Albert Hamm, the drummer; Johnny Toogood the invisible guitarist; Dave "Lazybones" Bartholomew the double bassist and Ronnie "Fingers" Ryan the pianist."

"How did you know their names?"

"I had an informant, a mole on the inside."

"Cornelius?"

"No, he's obviously our chief suspect. I wouldn't ask him."

"Well, who then?"

"Me, of course." A lady at a neighbouring table on the other side of the partition stood up and smiled at them. "Do you mind if I join you?"

"Alice. Alice Aylesbeare. What are you doing here?" Ella was pleased to see her old friend.

"I am proud to be the Secretary of the CIA."

"Gosh, you are really deep undercover."

"You haven't even got an American accent."

"No, the CIA is Corn's International Appreciatives. It's his worldwide fan club. Or at least, it used to be. Most of our members are OAPs living in places like Bexhill on Sea."

"Or Budleigh Salterton?" added Ella.

"We've got a couple of members in Australia, one more in New Zealand, and even a pensioner in Darkest Peru."

"A relative of Paddington Bear?"

"I don't think so. I've never met or spoken to her. She does, however, live in a retirement home in Lima so, on reflection, she could be."

"We also have a president that you may remember."

"Don't tell me," said Ella, "Amelia Nutwell."

"How did you know? She's a name from your recent

past, isn't she?"

"Yes, we've met!"

"Well, welcome Alice," smiled Frank. "Once again we seem to be assisting the police with their enquiries!"

"Of course. And one more thing, I don't appreciate being called a mole. I have very good vision for a Budleigh Saltertonite."

Alice brought her drink and her dessert over to the table. "I'm afraid I'm a little ahead of you," she apologised.

"That's not a problem. I'd better leave room for dessert. It looks delicious!"

"Back to the suspects, please," said Elsie, attempting to bring some order once more to the proceedings.

"Right. We've got Cornelius and all the band members," said Ella.

"Jane the third wife and Annie Saxon," added Frank.

"Yes, Jane turned up before the first murder. She said she wandered around the village, but can she prove it?" Ella used her finger to tick off her name on an imaginary blackboard.

"And Annie Saxon keeps turning up at the scenes of the crimes although not necessarily at the correct time!" Frank copied his wife.

"The butler. What's his name?" asked Elsie.

"Reeves," Ella informed her.

"He's worth investigating. Has he got a back story?" Elsie jotted down some words in her notebook.

"Any other suspects," wondered Ella.

"The chef, Emanuel. Although he never seems to leave his kitchen. There's also the two sisters, Mary and Martha. They live in the village."

"We'll include them, but we need to find a motive."

"Perhaps Emanuel met Cornelius on a Spanish tour? Or he's had an affair with each one of the wives? Or…"

"We're straying again. Any more suspects?"

"You two," said Alice pointing at Frank and Ella.

Frank shook his head. "No, maybe the first murder but not the second. We were nowhere near Lyme Regis. We spent the evening in the hotel. One of the band even phoned us at the hotel on the hotel phone to ask us if Betty had arrived back."

"That seems a reasonable alibi - this time," replied Alice with a twinkle in her eye.

"We've got three more suspects to add to the list," volunteered Ella.

"Who?" asked Alice.

"The remaining three wives. We've accounted for three of the wives. That leaves us with another three."

"The six wives of Henry the Eighth?"

"In this case Cornelius Spooner. Doesn't quite have the same ring to it."

"Who are these wives? Alice, do you know anything about them?" asked Frank.

"No, but I'll try to find out. You'll want to know their names and their present whereabouts."

Ella added. "What about any grudges or jealousies that have built up. There's a good chance that one of them could be the murderer. They may be here right now. We just haven't met them yet."

"Any other suspects?" asked Elsie as she finished jotting down in her notebook.

"Not that we know of," said Frank. "It could be that someone has gathered all our suspects together in the hotel and is looking to bump them off one by one."

"Very Agatha Christie-ish," added Ella. "Just like that story she wrote that took place on Burgh Island. I'll need to re-read it to see what happened."

"I bet there's a copy in the hotel library." laughed Frank.

Alice ambled back to Budleigh to do some research whilst Elsie drove Frank and Ella back to the Cobb country House hotel.

Stepping inside the front door, they were confronted with two ladies having a stand-up row in Reception. Martha was trying to calm them down without any success.

The noise appeared to be growing louder by the second. Frank and Ella could make out snippets of the discussion.

"If we're here because of the money, then I'm entitled to far more of it than you."

"Why? You never did nothing. Just sponged off 'im."

"You take that back. That's an outrageous lie."

"The only outrageous fing is that dress of yours. If you're so 'ard up, why are you wearing that?"

"This is second hand from the local charity shop."

"Second 'and, my foot. Mutton dressed as...."

"L-A-D-I-E-S!!" A cacophonous, deafening voice interrupted them.

They both stopped and turned towards the source of the noise.

"Cornelius!!" They both shouted together.

"Good afternoon, Lydia. Good afternoon, Imelda."

Cornelius turned towards Frank and Ella.

"May I introduce to you Lydia, number four and Imelda, number five. My ex-wives!"

# CHAPTER 12

# LITTLE ARROWS

Ella was gob-smacked. Frank's face wore an amused smile.

"Four and five? Just how many wives have you got?" asked Ella even though she knew the answer.

"Six."

"Henry the Eighth! Must be your nickname?" Frank's face was an image of innocence.

Behind the Reception desk, Martha's smile was quickly removed when she noticed both ladies staring at her.

"Me key?" demanded Lydia.

"Almost exactly what I was going to say!" Imelda held out her hand towards Martha.

"You don't need keys. Use these instead." Martha handed both of them smart cards, informed them where their rooms were and with a curt but professional "Follow me" led them away from Reception and off to their rooms.

"Well, Cornelius," began Frank, "no wonder you're still touring. Your bank account must have quite a lot of outgoings."

Cornelius smiled but said nothing.

Ella was still trying to process the recent developments. She had so many questions. "Did you invite them down here and why? Do they know about your other wives? And what about the first two? I mean, they're not with us anymore, are they?"

Cornelius held up a hand like a traffic policeman on point duty. Ella noticed he was wearing six rings on his various fingers. All golden and unique. "Hold on a minute. You sound like that policewoman. To answer your first question. I did not invite them down here. I was surprised as…., I was surprised as anything to hear them as they were registering."

"But Diane and Betty?"

"I understand what you're saying. It isn't safe for them to be here."

"Exactly."

"In that case, I'll tell them to go back to their homes first thing tomorrow."

"Let's hope that's not too late," muttered Frank.

"I agree." Cornelius stood there thinking. "This whole week is proving to be horrendous. Worse than horrendous. I've never felt so bad, so helpless. I'm going to give all this up and… move abroad. Spain? Florida? Australia?"

The great Cornelius Spooner looked as if he were about to cry.

"I don't know what to do. I need a drink."

He turned his back on Frank and Ella and slumped off to the lounge.

"Either he's a brilliant actor or someone's setting him up." Frank and Ella made their way back to their room.

"Hello, Martha, isn't it? Can you help me?"

"Certainly, ma'am."

"Please, I'm Mrs. Spooner, Imelda Spooner. I'm looking for a walk with great views. Where can I go? Where do the locals go?"

"Cannington Viaduct, miss. It's a simple walk from here. Not too hilly. If you're really careful you can get on the viaduct and the views from there are stunning."

"Sounds perfect. How do I get there? Is there a map?"

"Yes, Mrs. Spooner. We've got some photocopied Ordnance Survey maps of the area. I'll get you one."

"That's most kind."

Martha searched underneath the counter.

"Here it is. I'll just draw the route."

Martha quickly pencilled in the route. "Here you are. Have a good ramble." Martha handed the photocopy to Imelda Spooner.

"Thank you."

The next morning, after breakfast, Frank and Ella were involved in an interesting discussion with Martha about the Rousdon Estate.

"The place used to belong to the Peek Family, the biscuit people."

"Ah yes, Peek Frean's biscuits. Custard Creams, Bourbon, Garibaldi!" Frank's taste buds had been activated.

"They invented them all. James Peek and George Frean started off making ship's biscuits in the 1850s and by the time James sold his share of the business they had diversified and employed over seven hundred people. They eventually merged with Huntley and Palmers. Now, it's part of Kraft Foods."

"How do you know all this?"

"We all had to do a project about it at school. Local history. I made the teacher some of their biscuits and won a prize. So, I suppose, the information stuck."

Frank and Ella nodded in admiration.

"Anyway," Martha went on, "James' son, Henry, bought the whole village of Rousdon, restored the church and school and then built a mansion near the Undercliff, overlooking the sea."

"We'd like to have a look around," said Frank.

"I don't know if you're allowed."

"Don't worry, Martha, we're not going to cause trouble - just curious, that's all."

"There's a footpath that crosses the Estate."

"I'm sure we'll keep to it."

Frank and Ella crossed the Lyme Regis road and made their way up the main drive. As it branched to the right towards the house, Frank and Ella took the left fork and made their way along a pathway, past East lodge and along the side of the house towards the sea. Eventually, they reached a car park at the head of a path that led downhill towards the sea.

"What goes down must come up!" mused Frank.

"Let's turn back, I'd like to explore around the main house. There looked like there were loads of other buildings."

They soon reached East Lodge and headed for the

mansion. It appeared to be Victorian with a brown tiled roof, many tall chimney stacks and red brick and flint frontage. There looked to be three floors and the upper floors had mock Tudor timbers.

"Look at all those windows!" Ella marvelled.

"Yes, if you were a window cleaner, you'd start at one end, make your way across and then straightaway have to go back and start all over again."

"A job for life!"

As they were gazing in wonderment at the scope of the mansion, they were approached by a man dressed in a tweed country jacket and wearing green Wellington boots.

"Good morning, may I help you?"

"Good morning," replied Frank non-committally.

"Are you interested in buying?"

"The mansion? No, a bit beyond our income bracket, I expect."

"No, madam, I meant, the cottages and other houses on the estate. Over there."

He pointed to the west of the mansion and through the trees, they could see plenty of smaller buildings.

"Although Peek House, part of the Mansion house, is for sale."

"How much?" asked Ella cheekily.

"Just about seven figures."

"We'll pass."

They started walking towards the trees.

"I didn't introduce myself. Paul Ellard, Estate Manager."

"Frank and Ella Raleigh," offered Frank. "We own Kennaway Coopers, over at Ottery."

"I've heard of your place. You produce excellent beer

barrels."

"That's us. Tell me," asked Frank, "does the Peek family still live here?"

"No, not for a long time. They sold it to a school just before the Second World War. Allhallows public school. They moved here from Honiton. In the 1970s it was one of the first public schools to admit girls. But, by the 1990s, it was in decline and it closed in 1998."

"Who owns it now?"

"The Allhallows Estate. A group of people bought it and invested in the place bringing it up to scratch. There are over a hundred houses on the Estate, 350 acres of cottages, big houses and holiday lets. It's an enclosed community. If you own a property here, then you can buy shares in the company and have a say in how it's managed."

"Sounds wonderful," sighed Ella.

"We're staying at the hotel. It's lovely but I'd rather stay here!"

"Well, if you're interested, I could always send you a brochure."

"Yes, please," said Ella.

They gave him their details and bid him farewell.

"You do know this is private property? Please stay on the main drive on your way back to the road."

"We will, Paul."

This time they did. They ambled back to the hotel in time for morning coffee.

For a sedate Country House Hotel, the lounge was bucking the trend. Frank and Ella could hear the shouting before they stepped through the front door.

"It's Lydia and Imelda and if I'm not mistaken, Jane as well," gasped Ella.

"All three wives in the same room? That's asking for trouble."

"Yes, you have enough problems with just one, let alone three," twinkled Ella.

Frank decided not to reply but moved towards the lounge. They both stood at the door watching the spectacle unfolding before their eyes.

The three women were surrounding Cornelius. He was trapped in the middle and whichever way he faced, he was forced to turn his back on one of his wives. Reeves, the butler stood by the coffee trolley tapping his feet.

Ella could have sworn he had the slightest of smiles on his face. "Is he enjoying this?" she asked Frank.

"I shouldn't think so. Piggy in the middle."

"Not Cornelius. I can see he's hating every second. No, I meant Reeves."

Frank's eyes drifted towards the butler. "No, I think he's a bit embarrassed."

Cornelius spotted Frank and Ella. His eyes were pleading for help.

Frank put on his school masterly voice. "Ladies!" he declared.

There was no response.

"Ladies," he repeated but louder.

The haranguing continued unabated.

Frank moved one of the wooden dining chairs and placed it in front of the door. He gingerly climbed up on it. Ella held him steady.

"Ladies," he shouted at the top of his voice. This time it

worked. They stopped and swivelled their bodies towards him.

"Thank you. We could hear you outside. In fact, the whole village could probably hear you. Now sit down on a chair. You, there!" He pointed Imelda towards a chair in one corner.

"And you, there," indicating Lydia towards the opposite corner.

"And you... there," signalling Jane towards the chair by the window.

Cornelius stood still in the middle of the room, unsure where to sit. "Cornelius, just stay there. Stand still and be quiet."

Amazingly all four of them obeyed him. Must be the school master in him. They moved to their allotted positions and peace returned to the lounge of the Cobb Country Hotel.

"Reeves," said Frank, turning towards the butler. "Perhaps you can explain what is going on?"

"Certainly, sir. It would appear that these ladies are rather annoyed with this gentleman." He nodded towards Cornelius.

"Why?" asked Ella.

"They all objected to the presence of the other ladies. They were under the impression that they were to be the solitary companion to the gentleman this week."

"Cornelius, perhaps you can enlighten us on your plans for these ladies?" asked Frank.

"I know nothing about it. I didn't invite them. Why would I? They're three, four and five. I've moved onto six. And she's not here."

Jane raised her hand. Frank nodded.

"That's all we were trying to find out. Why were we

here? And who did invite us?"

"And if it weren't Cornelius," added Lydia. "Then who were it?"

The atmosphere had calmed down. Ella helped Frank down from the chair before they both sat down on the spare sofa. Reeves handed out coffee. Cornelius still stood in the middle of the room.

"Sit down, Cornie," said Imelda.

"I'd like to but where?" He looked towards Frank for inspiration.

"Come and sit by us," said Ella. "I'm very happily married so you won't cause any trouble here, will you?"

"Er, no," murmured Cornelius.

Ella had never seen him looking so meek. Where had the showman, the pop star, the larger than life musical artiste gone?

"So, who invited you, then?" Ella asked Imelda.

"I received a typewritten letter through the post with a coach ticket and details of a booking for a room at this hotel."

"Same here," chorused Jane and Lydia.

"Who signed the letter?"

"It was unsigned," continued Imelda. Jane and Lydia nodded. "I just assumed it was Cornelius."

"Why?"

"Well, there was a newspaper cutting in the letter. It was a review from one of his gigs earlier in the tour."

Again, Jane and Lydia nodded.

"And you didn't invite them?" asked Ella, turning to Cornelius.

"No, why would I?"

"Why indeed?" mused Frank.

Reeves coughed. "If everyone has finished, then I need to prepare the dining room for lunch."

"Certainly," said Frank. He took his and Ella's cups and placed them on the trolley. The meeting broke up in a quieter frame of mind than it had been when Frank and Ella appeared.

They both made their way up to their room. When they closed their door behind them, they looked at each other and burst out laughing.

"What a to-do!" giggled Ella.

"None of this makes any sense to me at all."

"I agree. We've got two dead bodies. They may both have been murdered. But no one seems to care. Our two police friends have just left them alone. It's as if nothing has happened."

"We're staying in a mad house!"

"Let's get away - straight after lunch."

"Back to Otterbury?" Frank asked.

"No, I want to see what, if anything, happens next."

"Shall we go for a walk?"

"Yes, exactly what I need. I want to go back to that viaduct. I want to see if we can get on to it. The view would be marvellous."

Frank unravelled a map and consulted it.

"The Cannington viaduct. We can get to it from here. No need to take the car."

"Let's do that. Let's be adventurous explorers for the afternoon."

"Straight after lunch."

Frank's school-masterly tones were not needed in the

dining room. Lunch was a gentle, peaceful affair. Every guest attended. Politeness and civility were the order of the day. Even the band behaved themselves. The food, as usual, was delicious and plentiful. Whatever deficiencies existed in the situation, it had nothing to do with the hotel and its fare.

Frank and Ella excused themselves and were soon on their way towards the Cannington Viaduct. They left the hotel and sauntered northwards along Green Lane past the farmhouse with its imposing chimneys and its multitudinous outbuildings before continuing on the footpath at the end of the lane. They turned right when the footpath came out on a narrow tarmacked road. Eventually, they reached a crossroads. Consulting their map, they crossed over and carried on. The hedgerows were alive with ferns and wildflowers. Trees regularly provided shade and shelter from the sun. They passed an area of woodland that appeared to be poorly maintained. Rotten branches littered the woodland floor.

"Somewhere to our left is the route of the old railway. It's been dismantled, of course. But it looks as if we can follow the old track bed."

Sure enough, they tiptoed over a cattle grid and there was the old railway track, now a dusty farm track. They turned off the empty road and began strolling along what was once the permanent way. The road fell away on their right-hand side down into a grassy valley dotted with farm buildings and sparse groups of trees. The track stayed on the level following the ridge. It was obvious a railway had run along its length. They could see the viaduct in the distance.

"Will we be able to walk over it?" asked Ella.

"Don't see why not. As long as it's safe."

As they approached the viaduct, their doubts grew.

"Looks like there's a gate blocking the bridge entrance."

"We can get through there easily."

"Why would they put gates here?"

"I don't know. Maybe to stop the bungee jumpers?"

"Or the suicides?"

"How could you kill yourself with this view?"

They scrambled past the iron gates and onto the viaduct. The track bed was overgrown with weeds, small trees and brambles.

"It looks in pretty ropey condition. What's this viaduct made of?"

"Concrete, I think."

They moved carefully to the viaduct parapet and looked out over the valley. The bridge groaned with their movement.

"I think we should keep well clear of the parapet. This place doesn't seem to like visitors."

They moved back to the relative safety of the track bed. They could still clearly see the glory of the surrounding countryside.

"What a stunning view!" gasped Ella.

"It's a long way down."

"I have no intention of going down. I'm no bungee jumper and life is too precious to throw it away."

Frank and Ella spent some minutes gazing around. "Look," Frank muttered. "There's someone else on the bridge at the far end."

"They look familiar."

Ella stared discretely to the other end of the bridge.

"It's Imelda. Wife number five. What's she doing here?"

"Probably out for an explore, like us."

Ella decided not to make her way towards Imelda. Instead, she waved her hands and shouted, "Hi, Imelda. Lovely view!"

Imelda immediately turned her back on the pair and disappeared through the gate at the eastern end of the bridge.

"How strange?"

"Perhaps she wants some time alone," added Frank. "It's probably been a bit of an ordeal for her - this last day or so."

Ella took one last perusal of the panoramic view.

"Time to head back, I think. Don't want to miss afternoon tea. Who knows what might happen!"

*Ah, there she is.*

*Where's she going?*

*Oh, this is going to be too easy. Just stay there, little lady.*

*Just stay by the target.*

*Yes, have a look and see what it's made of. It's a hay bale with a paper target pinned on it.*

*Right, concentrate.*

*These gloves are no good. Need to wipe the bow afterwards thoroughly.*

*Bolt in place?*

*Calling card at the ready?*

*Don't worry, little lady.*

*Don't you just love how naive they are?*

*You won't feel a thing. Well, not much anyway.*

*A little scream and the deed is done.*

*Sweet dreams.*
*Drum roll, please. Bullseye.*

# CHAPTER 13

# STUCK IN THE MIDDLE
# WITH YOU

"I found her over there. Just lying. She had been shot with a crossbow. Good shot, too. The bolt went straight through the heart. I expect she didn't feel a thing."

Reeves the butler looked a little less than his usual calm, collected self.

Sergeant Knowle quietly looked at him and allowed him to continue.

"I was doing the rounds of the garden to announce the commencement of afternoon tea. I saw her lying there in front of the target. Do you think someone shot her by accident? It's awful. The reputation of our hotel will be in tatters if this gets out."

PC Hydon coughed and finished off taking notes.

"Thank you, Jeeves, er, Reeves. That will be all for now."

Reeves moved silently away towards the main house. Sergeant Knowle stared at PC Alf Hydon. "I think his hotel's reputation will be in tatters now the papers have found out."

"Sorry, ma'am. My fault, I guess."

"How?"

"It must have slipped out last night at the Three Horseshoes. I only had 'alf a pint of Sowdon's. I was talking to a lovely lady in the snug. I warn't to know she was from the newspaper."

"And now we have a small crowd of them at the front gate."

"Does that mean we'll be taken off the case?"

"Not yet. I've persuaded Exeter to give me today to discover as much as I can."

They stopped as the scene of crime people, all three of them, arrived. Sergeant Knowle told them what she knew, and they immediately sprang into action.

"Three murders. Phew!" sighed PC Hydon. "They'll have our guts for garters if we darn't produce some results and quickly."

"Well, we haven't done too well so far. Where are Frank and Ella? Perhaps they've got more idea about this."

"I'll go and find them, straightway," volunteered PC Hydon, glad to get away from the scene relatively unscathed.

Frank and Ella found a pathway into the hotel that led through the gardens. They saw Elsie Knowle and approached her with weary smiles on their faces.

"It's a long walk back from Cannington Viaduct," Ella began.

Sergeant Elsie Knowle pointed towards the body lying in front of the archery target.

"Oh no, not another one!" Ella fell to her knees in anguish. "Who is it?"

Elsie knelt down beside her. "We think it's Jane Spooner, Cornelius' third wife."

"First Diane, then Betty and now Jane." Even Frank sat down on the grass and looked to be on the verge of tears.

"I don't know if we can stay here any longer, Elsie. It's not safe. Three murders? We could all be killed, one by one. It's like that Agatha Christie story, only this is for real."

The three of them lapsed into silence as they tried to take in the enormity of the situation.

"No," said Ella breaking into the silence. "It's our responsibility to help Elsie and Alf solve these crimes. If that *is* Jane, and if she *was* murdered, then I'm going to try my very best to bring her murderer to justice."

"Could it have been an accident?" asked Frank as he blew his nose with his handkerchief.

"Any of the three deaths *could* have been an accident," replied Elsie. "But I don't think so. This is murder and I think we have a serial killer here in this hotel. I'm sure Exeter would rather bring in Scotland Yard, but I'm going to apprehend our killer if it's the last thing I do."

Both Frank and Ella were stunned by Elsie's passionate response.

"Right, Elsie. If you want our help, we'd be honoured to stay and assist," said Frank recovering his poise.

"Excellent. I think I'm going to need all the help I can get." They stood up and watched as the scene of crime personnel finished their gruesome jobs.

Frank and Ella went to their room to get changed. Half an hour later they met Ella back out in the gardens. She was sitting on the garden seat by the maze.

"Let me fill you in on what I know. I'm told she was shot through the heart with a crossbow bolt. The crossbow is lying in the bushes over there. Reeves the butler found the body and the crossbow. He looked almost human when he told me. He was verging on the edge of being flustered. Still, he ended up being more concerned about the reputation of this hotel. He's a strange one."

"Typical butler, though," added Frank.

"Yes, you're right. I bet he was born a butler, went to butler school and will die a butler. They'll bury him in his uniform and white gloves!"

Ella smiled, then frowned. "I'm trying not to picture Reeves in his coffin."

"Sorry, a bit tasteless," apologised Elsie. "Let me continue."

"We've now accounted for everybody including you two. Except for Cornelius. He's not on the premises. No-one's seen him since lunchtime."

"Is Imelda here?"

"If you mean wife number five. Yes, she's here. Why?"

"Well, we thought we saw her at Cannington Viaduct," answered Frank.

"That's where we've been for a walk," added Ella.

"OK, I'll double-check that. I've spoken to everyone including Imelda."

Elsie produced her notebook.

"I've spoken briefly to Johnny Flynn, Johnny Toogood, Davy Bartholomew, Ronnie Ryan, Lydia Spooner, Imelda Spooner, Reeves the butler, Martha the waitress and Emanuel the cook."

"And…?"

"They were all on their own between the end of lunch and when Jane was shot."

"So any of them could have done it? Yet again."

"Yes, and they're all scared witless, particularly the remaining Spooners."

"Wives number four and five?"

Their conversation was interrupted by an anxious-looking PC Alf Hydon.

"'xcuse me for butting in. Oi just thought you should know about that little crowd at the front gate."

"Good. Have they all dispersed?"

"No. Quite the opposite. There's more of them. More journalists and now more of Cornelius' fans. There's a group of rubber-neckers and…"

"Rubber-neckers?" queried Ella.

"Yes, you know." Alf did an impression of something that resembled an emu on steroids.

"Right, we need to call in reinforcements," ordered Elsie.

"Already done that. We've got ten special constables on their way from Sidmouth, Honiton and Axminster."

"Well done. Good thinking."

"And I read the riot act to the whole crowd. Warned them that if any of them put one little toe on the hotel's land, I'd arrest them for trespass and make sure they felt the full force of the law."

"Did that work? Did they buy it?" asked Frank.

"Surprisingly enough, yes. The journalists went back to their cars, got out some beach chairs and a crate of beer and parked themselves at the front gates. Some of the villagers even turned around and headed for home."

"Good."

"Well, not really."

"Don't tell me," said Frank, "they came back with their own chairs."

"Exactly. Some even brought primus stoves. One of them

brought a tent. They're here for the long haul."

"Right, PC Hydon. Get back to the gates and make sure everything is secure."

"Yes, ma'am."

"Frank, Ella. How did you get back into the hotel grounds?"

"We used the back gate. Same way as we left."

"Is that the only other way in or out?"

"I think so," said Ella.

"I'm going to tour the perimeter fence and check for myself. We need to make this place secure."

Frank and Ella looked at each other. "I think we're in for a siege!"

Frank and Ella went into the lounge for afternoon tea. The room was empty. There was no tea trolley, no Reeves and no guests. Frank looked outside towards the front gates. The Special Constables had arrived and secured the premises. They both stood in silence for several minutes, consumed in their thoughts.

Ella broke the silence. "Where is everyone?" Frank was startled out of his cogitations. "In England, we've been through a civil war, the Great Fire of London, the plague, two world wars and a World Cup win."

"Yet," added Ella, "everything always stops for tea." She tried very hard to keep a straight face.

Frank smirked. Ella joined him. They collapsed onto the sofa by the window and the smirks burgeoned into fits of giggles.

"Seriously," Frank said a few minutes later. "I expect they're all in their rooms hiding away."

"Shouldn't we be doing the same?"

"No, I don't think the murderer is after us. It's all connected somehow with Cornelius. Either he's gone mad and is reaping revenge on his wives or someone else has gone mad and is reaping revenge on him."

"Either way, you don't think we're in danger?"

"No, I think our murderer is so fixed on their victims that they haven't even thought about the consequences of their actions. I bet they don't even think about anyone trying to stop them!"

"Whoever it is, they're extremely twisted."

"Yes, which is why we need to catch them before anyone else is killed. I think we're safer out in the open, sticking together and covering each other's backs!"

Ella nodded. "Have we got any more clues?"

As she asked Frank, the door opened and in walked Sergeant Elsie Knowle.

"Yes, as a matter of fact, *we* do have another clue."

"Another card?"

"Yes, how did you guess?"

"Well, if the murders are all linked, then there has to be another card."

Ella looked at Elsie. "Remind me what the cards have been so far."

"Well, first of all, there was:

*Ding, dong, bell,*

*Pussy's in the well.*

*Who put her in?*

*Little Johnny Flynn.*"

"A simple nursery rhyme," mused Ella. "Surely the pussy was Diane. But who is little Johnny Flynn?"

"Then there was Betty down in Lyme Regis on the Cobb,"

added Elsie.

*"I'd like to be under the sea*

*In an octopus's garden in the shade*

*He'd let us in, knows where we've been*

*In his octopus's garden in the shade"* read Elsie from her notebook.

"Well, she was certainly under the sea," agreed Frank.

"Perhaps the octopus's garden has something to do with it?" replied Elsie.

"The tentacles of the past reaching out through time?" voiced Frank.

"Very symbolic! What does the third card say?"

Elsie again consulted her notebook.

*"Robin Hood, Robin Hood, riding through the glen*

*Robin Hood, Robin Hood, with his band of men*

*Feared by the bad, loved by the good*

*Robin Hood, Robin Hood, Robin Hood."*

"I watched that program when I was a young boy. It started in the Fifties. I saw the repeats on Children's TV in the Sixties. *The Adventures of Robin Hood.* Richard Greene as Robin and Alan Wheatley as the Sheriff of Nottingham. Amazing how those childhood memories stick around," stated Frank.

"The murderer sees themselves as a kind of Robin Hood feared by the bad?"

"Is Robin Cornelius? Reeves? One of the band? Perhaps a woman? Like a pantomime leading boy?"

"What about the band of men?"

"Are they all in it together?"

"No, some of them are too young to remember the Sixties," Frank said with a smile.

"Just because you can."

"Actually, just because you can't remember the Sixties doesn't mean you weren't there."

"I assume," said Elsie in a stern voice, "That's some kind of drug reference. I'm not sure you should be making such comments!"

Frank smiled again. "Loved by the good?" he said returning to the subject of the conversation.

"I can't think of any good person who would love a serial murderer," replied Elsie. She once again consulted her notebook. "And on the reverse of each card, the words 'Best wishes. Cornelius.'"

"Would he really sign each card?" asked Frank.

"No, unless it's some sort of double bluff."

"And why a full stop and not a comma?"

"Not this again!" laughed Ella.

The three of them sat there in momentary silence gathering their thoughts.

Ella sighed. "We're finding more and more questions and fewer and fewer answers!"

There was a knock on the lounge door and without waiting for a reply, PC Alf Hydon lumbered in.

"Bad news, ma'am," he blurted out.

"Not another body?"

"No, nothing like that. We've just had Inspector Wilkins again at the front gate. He was sent by Exeter to lead the investigation."

"Good," said Elsie. "They're taking it seriously!"

"No, not good. There's been a major incident back in Exeter. The Assistant Chief Constable told him personally to return to Exeter and take charge of it. He hadn't even had a chance to get out of his car. He did have a message for you, though."

"Who did, Inspector Wilkins?"

"No, the Assistant Chief Constable."

"What did he have to say?"

"He said and I quote…" PC Alf Hydon took out his notebook and opened it at his latest page of scribblings. "He said - I have every confidence in you and your select team to solve these series of accidents."

"That's very good of him…" began Ella.

"He *still* isn't taking it seriously!" Sergeant Elsie Knowle was not happy.

"There's more."

"Go on."

"I hear," he read, "that Frank and Ella Raleigh are staying at the hotel. See if they can help?"

Elsie stood in the centre of the room and surveyed the other three with an uncompromising expression. She voiced what Frank, Elsie and Alf were thinking. "These are not accidents. I think we're going to have to remain here until we solve these murders. It has to be a person staying in this hotel or one of the staff."

Frank smiled once again. "I think that's a very good idea. With the police here, we may just stop this murderer from killing any more of Cornelius' wives."

Ella was staring out of the window when her mobile phone started quietly buzzing. "I changed the ringtone just in case it disturbed any important conversations."

"I think you should change it to a piercing alarm. Might come in useful!" said Frank.

Ella ignored him and held the phone to her ear. "Hello,

Alice! Any news?"

"Where is she?" mouthed Frank.

Ella switched on the speaker phone.

"I'm out the back of the hotel near the maze. There's a very large special constable on patrol by the back gate and she wouldn't let me in."

"I don't think you should be in here, Alice. It's all getting a little bit tense," replied Ella. "You stay on the outside and we'll let you know if we need anything. If you get in here, you may not be allowed out again!"

"Yes, I thought you might like me to stay on the outside. I've found a few things of interest. I've printed them up and bundled them together. Go out to the maze and look up at the sky."

"Are you going to throw them over the hedges?"

"I'm not that good at cricket and I'm not doing a pole vault! But I've found another way to get them in. Bye!"

There was a brief buzzing noise as Alice ended the call.

"What was that all about?"

"Let's head to the maze!"

Frank, Ella, Elsie and Alf walked swiftly out of the hotel and around to the maze area. As they arrived, they heard the same buzzing noise that they had heard at the end of the phone call.

"Well, I'm blowed. Look upalong!" PC Alf pointed to the sky above the maze.

A drone with four wings extruding at right angles was airborne and headed their way. It looked to be carrying some form of luggage bag on the body of the craft.

"Watch out," shouted Alf. "It's looking unsteady."

"Oh my," cried Frank, "It's going to crash."

The craft veered off at a steep angle and aimed for the

maze. There was the sound of a muffled thump and the buzzing ceased.

"It's somewhere in the maze. Let's get after it," shouted Ella.

"Wait a minute," called Elsie. "We need some organisation. Frank and Ella, you two go in there. One go one way and one the other. I'll stand guard. PC Hydon here, will find an upstairs vantage point."

"Can't I use the lookout post?"

"No, that's slap bang in the middle of the maze. We don't want three of you in there."

"Yes, ma'am. I'll find a look out post in the hotel." PC Hydon briskly walked off across the lawn.

"If you need directing or get lost just wave your arms about and he'll let us know what to do and where to turn. PC Hydon has a very loud voice when the occasion warrants it."

Frank and Ella made their way into the maze and soon split up. Sergeant Knowle stood on guard at the entrance. PC Hydon stood for a moment surveying the windows on this side of the hotel before dashing indoors.

Sergeant Knowle waited patiently for him to appear at a window but after five minutes his face never appeared.

"Where is that man?" she muttered.

Her question was answered when for the second time in a very short time, PC Alf Hydon blundered back onto the scene.

"Where have you been?"

"Elsie, er, Ma'am, er, Sergeant Knowle. I think you should come at once. Oi think I've caught our killer."

# CHAPTER 14

# SOMETHING IN THE AIR

Frank and Ella made their way towards the last known sighting of the drone. Now and again they saw each other on the other side of an intervening hedge.

"Any luck?"

"No, what about you?"

"I think the finder should shout very loudly so the others know!"

"Good idea, Frank."

"Au-revoir!"

Ten minutes later Frank heard a loud cry from somewhere close by. "Ella, is that you?"

"Yes, I've found it. It did a nosedive and landed embedded in one of the hedges. I'm near the middle of the maze."

"Keep talking. I'll try and get as close as I can."

"I've gathered up the luggage. There are two bags. I'm opening up one of them and, my word, there's not much in here. Some photos, some Alice notes and a few printouts from some websites."

"Anything about the wives?"

"Oh yes, marriage dates, divorce dates. Oh, that's interesting!"

"What?"

"Oh, you sound much nearer now."

"I am. I'm on the other side of the hedge. I can see one of the drone's propellers sticking through."

"Oh, hello." She could see Frank's outline through the hedge. "Nice to see you."

"To see you nice!"

Ella giggled.

"Can you pull the drone out of the hedge?" Frank asked.

"Not really. But I think, I might be able to push it through to you."

There was a period of silence as Ella pushed.

"Keep going. It's coming through."

"What about you. Are you pulling as well?"

"I am and…."

Frank fell backwards as the drone came clear of the hedge and landed on top of him.

"You all right?" Ella asked.

"No harm done. Have you got the bags? They're not with the drone."

"Yes, all safe with me. Let's get back to the maze entrance."

"How?" asked Frank.

"Weren't you taking note of your directions?"

"No, of course not. Weren't you?"

"Too intent on the drone."

Frank heard Ella sigh.

Frank put on an over the top Scottish accent "We're

marooned. Marooned, I say. We're all doomed!!"

"Thank you, Fraser!" laughed Ella.

"Seriously though, this reminds me of a conversation I once had in the middle of the maze at Hampton Court. We'd been there on a school trip and I took a group of children into the maze. When we eventually reached the centre, the children were exhausted. They all sat down and refused to budge. An old man wandered into the centre of the maze and took one look at the children and turned to me. He stage-whispered that he knew of a short cut out of the maze. The children heard him and they all stood up waiting for him to continue. He turned back towards where he had come from and put his right hand out onto the hedge on his right. Looking over his shoulder, he stared at me and muttered, 'Simply keep your right hand in contact with the hedge. Follow the hedge and it will take you back to the start.' So, we took his advice, and in a line, one behind the other, we kept our right hands on the hedge and followed it."

"Did it work?"

"Let's find out."

Sergeant Knowle followed PC Hydon back into the hotel, through the dining room and reception hallway and out of the front door. One of the Special Constables was standing with a distraught looking lady.

"Lydia Spooner, ma'am," announce PC Hydon. "Wife number four. Our murderer!"

"Hello, Lydia," uttered Sergeant Knowle. "Perhaps we can go back into the lounge for a little chat."

Frank and Ella were slowly but surely making their way out of the maze.

"This is a long shortcut," shouted Ella when she realised Frank was somewhere in the vicinity.

"But, at least, it's guaranteed to get us out."

"According to an old man who you *say* you met in Hampton Court. Sounds like a shaggy dog story!"

"It's a true story!"

"Yes, I think you were fooled. I expect he was a young man when he went in the maze."

"Alf!! Elsie!! Can you hear me?" bellowed Frank.

There was no reply.

Frank raised his arms above his head.

"Alf! Can you see my arms? Alf. Are we near the maze entrance yet?"

There was no reply.

"Marooned!" came the cry from a nearby hedge.

"Elsie!! Are you there?"

"Frank, I don't think they are there. Has something happened?"

"They wouldn't leave us alone in here. Not with a killer on the loose."

"I thought you said we'd be safe from the killer?"

"Being lost in a maze can play funny tricks on your mind."

"Thanks, Frank. Your job is to keep me safe when I need to be. And now, I need to be kept safe and you're not there by my side."

"Oh yes, I am. At your service, madam." Ella turned a corner in the maze to find Frank standing in front of her, one hand on the hedge on the other side to Ella's hand.

"Wait a minute," cried Ella. "Your hand is on my left hand side, the opposite side to mine."

"Yes, I suppose it depends on which way we were facing when we started."

"Gobbledeegook, bunkum and balderdash."

"Sounds like a firm of solicitors," laughed Frank. "Don't panic."

"I think I have every right to panic. We're lost in a maze, there's a killer on the loose and our police escort has gone AWOL."

"But I am here - your knight in shining armour. Follow me and I promise I'll get you out of here safely."

"Yeah, so you say!"

Frank snorted then turned on his heels and marched off.

Ella hurriedly followed. "Wait for me…"

As she turned the corner, she found herself at the entrance to the maze.

"You knew!!"

"I admit I may have had an inkling where the entrance was. I got there about a minute before we met up."

"Oh Frank!" Ella threw one of the bags at him and sat herself down wearily on the grass outside the maze entrance.

Lydia Spooner sat on one of the sofas in the lounge. Sergeant Knowle sat alongside her and PC Hydon stood over by the window taking notes.

"Now, Mrs. Spooner. Lydia. Tell us what you told the policeman at the front gates."

"Certainly. I killed Diane, Betty and Jane."

"How did you kill Diane?"

"That was easy. I met 'er walking along the road through the village. As she turned away, I hit 'er over the head with me handbag. She fell rather awkwardly and must have hit 'er head on the road surface."

"But she was…" PC Hydon started to say.

"Be quiet, PC Hydon," Sergeant Knowle raised her hand to remonstrate.

Alf immediately shut up.

"Please continue, Lydia."

"I dragged 'er back to the hotel and dumped 'er down the well. No-one saw me."

"Why did you kill her?"

"She deserved it. When I was married to poor Cornelius, she was always demanding money from 'im."

Sergeant Knowle could hear PC Hydon furiously scribbling.

"What about Betty?"

"Same. I saw 'er in the village. I hit 'er. This time, I just left 'er there. Someone was coming so I scarpered."

"And Jane?"

"Well, I saw 'er behaving like Lady Muck so I got hold of a bow and arrow and shot 'er. Good shot, wasn't it?"

"It certainly must have been, Lydia."

"What's going to 'appen to me?"

"Well, I don't know. I think for now, you should go up to your room and have a little nap. The nice police constable and myself will take you to your room. I will put the nice police constable on guard outside your door to make sure you don't escape."

PC Hydon and Sergeant Knowle looked at each other knowing exactly what the other was thinking. They gently took Lydia Spooner upstairs to her room and settled her down. She offered no resistance. PC Hydon found a comfortable chair, positioned it outside her door and settled down on guard.

Sergeant Knowle stood in the corridor. "Are you quite comfortable?"

"Oh yes, ma'am." Then PC Hydon quickly stood up. "Sorry ma'am!"

"Don't worry. I'll send one of the Special constables up here later to relieve you."

"I'm just wondering, ma'am. Who am I guarding and who am I keeping safe?"

"Where are Elsie and Alf?" asked Ella. The lawn around the maze was deserted and no policeman's helmet could be seen projecting from any of the hotel windows.

Frank just shrugged. "Something must have dragged them away from here."

"Not another murder, please, not another murder."

Frank and Ella made their way rapidly back into the hotel. Ella went to search for Elsie whilst Frank deposited the drone and his bag in their room. He found PC Hydon stretched out on a well-padded chair in one of the hotel corridors.

"Are you enjoying some time off?" Frank queried.

"No, Frank, oi'm on guard. Mrs. Spooner's inside her room. Resting."

"Which Mrs. Spooner?" inquired Frank.

"Mrs. Lydia. She's gone a bit funny like. She started telling me that she was the killer!"

"And you believed her?"

"Yes, at first. But her story don't add up. I suggest you

find ma'am, er, Sergeant Knowle. She'll fill you in on all the discrepancies."

"Whilst you're staying here…" Frank raised an eyebrow.

Alf finished his sentence. "On guard!"

Sergeant Knowle and Ella were standing outside the front of the Cobb Country House Hotel surveying the scene at the front gates.

"There's more of them now. Journalists. Sightseers. Villagers. There's even a TV crew. Just a local one at the moment."

"Well, at least, they can't get in."

"No, the fence around the hotel is pretty secure. There's only two gates and we've got our Special Constables stationed at both."

"They can't get in and we can't get out," murmured Ella.

"That's about the long and short of it."

Frank appeared on the scene. "A stand-off?"

"Yes, and we're just dilly-dallying waiting for something to happen."

"I hear you had a confession?"

"Yes, that was from Lydia. That's why we had to leave you to get out of the maze on your own. You seem to have managed that without any problem."

"We just followed our hands."

"What?" Sergeant Knowle looked bemused.

"Never mind, Elsie. Long story. Tell us about Lydia's confession. Alf seemed to think she wasn't telling the truth."

"Let's go indoors, you two, and I'll tell you more."

They seated themselves once more in the lounge. It was becoming their office.

"She approached Alf, PC Hydon, as he was taking up his position of maze watcher. He came out to the maze to get me and we went to hear what she had to say. She seemed vague, almost drugged. Told us she killed Diane in the village by hitting her over the head and then she dragged the body all the way back to the hotel before dumping her in the well."

"Impossible!"

"Exactly, Ella. Then she continued by telling us she killed the second wife, Betty, in precisely the same manner. This time she just left her in the village."

"But," interrupted Frank, "Betty was found at the Cobb in Lyme Regis. Drowned not hit over the head."

"That's what the reports say. And that's what I believe."

"And then she killed Jane with a bow and arrow."

"Not a crossbow and dart?"

Ella looked alarmed. "Do you think she's having some mental health issues?"

"I think you've hit the nail on the head…. Er, poor choice of words. Sorry." Elsie almost blushed. "What I mean to say, is yes. I think the pressure of being the next in line, so to speak, has disturbed the balance of her mind."

Ella sat there taking it all in. "Perhaps she thought if she confessed, the police would take her away and keep her safe somewhere in a nice cosy jail cell, whilst you go about catching the real murderer."

"That's doesn't sound like the mind of a mad woman. Makes perfect sense to me." Frank was interrupted by a knock at the door and Reeves appeared with the tea trolley.

"Excuse me, ladies and gentleman, but I thought you

may require some refreshment. It's a hot day and so much has been going on."

"Yes, thank you, Reeves. Most considerate," said Elsie.

"I couldn't help overhearing about the fourth Mrs. Spooner. Perhaps a pot of tea for her as well?"

"Excellent idea. Bring it here and I'll take it up to her."

"I could do that, ma'am. Is she in her room?"

"Yes, but don't you worry about that. Bring the tea here on a tray and we'll do the rest."

Reeves left the tea trolley in the middle of the room and silently exited.

Tea on a tray duly arrived and the three of them prepared to continue the interview with Lydia. As they were about to leave the room, Frank put his hand on Ella's arm.

"I don't think it's a wise idea for all three of us to talk to Lydia. She'll feel outnumbered. I think you and Elsie should ask the questions. But there is one thing I'd like to know. Has she got any stories of Cornelius from the old days? How far back did their relationship go?"

"Just the two of us? I think you're right. A pot of tea and a nice ladies' chin wag."

Elsie and Ella left the room leaving Frank to sink into the sofa and his own thoughts.

They found Lydia sitting on the bed staring out of the window of her room. Her hands gripping the iron bedstead tightly.

Ella smiled. "We've brought you some tea."

"Thank you."

Sergeant Knowle sat on a chair by the window. Ella perched herself on the other side of the bed and started to break the ice. "So you were Cornelius' fourth wife, yes?"

"That's correct."

"Where did you meet him?"

"At some party in London."

"Was that in his hit-making days in the sixties?"

"Certainly not. No, this was in the late seventies. 'e was still a star. 'e sang pop tunes with rhythm. Glam rock without the glam. 'e was gorgeous. A real star. And our eyes met across the room. It was like 'e snapped 'is fingers and I just walked across the room and started dancing with 'im. It was love at first sight."

"Was he married then?"

"Yeah, to Jane Spooner. She was lovely looking but didn't have a clue 'ow to look after 'im."

"And you did?"

"Of course."

Ella poured a cup of tea for Lydia. She took it and gulped it down.

"What was he like then?" asked Elsie.

"Oh, with 'his musicians 'e was an 'ard taskmaster. But with me, 'e was a true gentleman."

"Hard taskmaster," repeated Elsie.

"Yeah, everyone 'ad to do the songs 'is way. If they missed a beat or played a wrong note, 'e'd fine them. Even if it was 'is fault, they'd be to blame. Whatever their excuse was, they'd be to blame."

"I bet a lot of the musicians didn't like that?"

"Course not. But what could they do? It was shut up or get out."

"And did they?"

"What d'yer mean? Yeah, some of them shut up. They took the money and knew their place. Others argued and they left. Either 'e sacked them, or they walked."

Lydia lapsed into silence. Ella and Elsie exchanged glances.

"Another cup of tea, Lydia?"

Lydia passed her cup to Ella who provided her with a refill.

"One time, I 'eard, there was a row 'bout 'is biggest 'it."

"*The Night is Still Young*?"

"Yeah, you know it. Yeah, I s'pose it's more your era than mine."

Ella ignored the unintended insult. "Tell me about it."

"Well, according to the credits, the song was written by Cornelius. 'E earned a fortune over the years from it. But I 'eard…"

Lydia looked around the room as if expecting intruders. "I 'eard 'e never wrote it. Someone else did. 'Is drummer at the time."

"And did the drummer complain?"

"Course 'e did. But 'e signed some sort of contract and 'e got a measly fee and not a penny more."

"So somewhere in the world there's a very angry drummer?"

"Yeah, suppose so. But it was a long time ago. I 'spect 'e's dead now."

Lydia lapsed once again into silence.

"Look, I'm a bit fed up staying cooped up in 'ere. Can I go for a walk?"

"I'd prefer it if you didn't," Elsie replied.

"Well, what about a book? There's a library 'ere, ain't there?"

"Yes," said Ella. "Shall I get you one, what do you like reading?"

"No, can I go? I'll only be a short while. Look, that copper outside the door can go with me."

Reluctantly, Elsie agreed. It was a decision she regretted for the rest of her life.

# CHAPTER 15

# POISON ARROW

Aargh, there she is.

You must be thirsty. Have a sip of this?

No?

Maybe hungry? Please take one. One bite 'll do.

Calling card at the ready. Rats, where is it?

Getting a little careless, aren 't we?

Slip it under the door. No one will notice.

Right, concentrate.

Gloves on?

Capsules at the ready?

Don 't worry, little lady.

Don 't you just love how stupid they are?

You won 't feel a thing. Well, not much anyway.

Drum roll, please. A little light refreshment, and it 's lights out for you.

Lydia, accompanied by PC Hydon, headed for the library. Both Ella and Elsie stood up and stretched.

"I'm glad they left the door open. It's getting pretty stuffy in here."

"I'll open a window," added Elsie.

Ella and Elsie resumed their seats and compared notes.

"Was there anything in her stories about Cornelius that might give a murderer a motive?" wondered Elsie.

"I don't know. Alice has done some research for us about his wives. That might shed some light. I've got some of it in this bag."

"Is that from the drone?"

"Yes, I've been carrying it around since we got out of the maze."

Ella put the bag down on the table by the tea tray.

"Anything that can help us would be gratefully received."

"Are you certain that Lydia was lying in her confessions?"

"Yes, she could have got some information about the first murder from the newspapers or from just asking anyone here in the hotel."

"She got the second murder completely wrong."

"I think she did that on purpose. Surely someone would have told her about both murders, not just the first one? And she never even mentioned Jane. Why wouldn't she claim to have shot her as well? No, I'm convinced she's not our murderer. But she is very, very scared of being victim number four." Elsie sounded more confident, the longer she spoke.

"I agree with you," Ella nodded. "I'm going to find Frank and go through Alice's bags with him. There's bound to be something of interest in one of them."

There was a loud knock on the door and Reeves came into the room without waiting to be asked.

"Excuse me for barging in, but PC Hydon has requested your assistance downstairs immediately."

"Where is he?" asked Sergeant Knowle, getting up and heading for the door.

"The Library, ma'am."

Both Ella and Sergeant Knowle rushed downstairs. The library door was open, and PC Hydon was on his knees cradling the prostrate body of Lydia Spooner on the library floor.

"Oh no," shouted the Sergeant. "What happened? Is she…"

"Dead, ma'am? No, I don't think so. She's breathing. It's very shallow but she's breathing. But she's unconscious. I've called for an ambulance. There's one on standby in Lyme Regis. It should be here…"

The distinct sound of an ambulance siren could be heard. Within a minute, two paramedics had entered the room. Ten minutes later, Lydia Spooner was in the ambulance and on the way to the nearest hospital.

"I should never have let her out of my sight!" Elsie slumped down into a library chair, head in her hands, on the verge of tears.

Frank joined his three shocked colleagues. Ella ushered him in. There were keys in both library doors, so she closed the doors and locked them.

"This is now a crime scene," she stated. "Don't move, look around you and see if you recognise any potentially incriminating evidence."

They all, including Elsie, took the time to see what was in the room.

Frank gave a running commentary. "There's books on the shelves. None of them appears to have been moved recently. They're not dusty but they all look ordered and cared for. The large table in the centre of the room, mahogany, I think, is surrounded by six high backed chairs, also mahogany. Apart from Elsie's chair, not one of them has been moved. Lydia fell onto the floor by that comfortable sofa. She knocked over a coffee table. And...."

"And on the floor," continued Elsie excitedly, "is a tray with an empty drinks cup and a spilt bottle of liquid."

"I'll get a sample of the liquid straightaway, ma'am," said PC Hydon. He burst into life taking out from one of his pockets a plastic evidence exhibit bag.

"Do that, please."

The other three continued their observations.

Ella continued. "There's a plate of biscuits over by the fireplace on that small wooden table next to the left-hand armchair. There's crumbs on the plate. I think someone has eaten, at least one of the biscuits."

All three of them turned towards PC Hydon.

"No, that wasn't me. Not on duty."

"Put those biscuits into another evidence exhibit bag as well."

PC Hydon finished labelling the first bag and then obeyed Sergeant Knowle's request.

"Anything else?" asked Ella.

"No, nothing obviously incriminating," said Frank.

"Well," continued Ella, "let's find out what happened after Lydia and PC Hydon left the bedroom. Can everyone please sit down around the table?"

When they were all seated, PC Hydon laid the evidence bags on the table. Seeing everyone was, once again, staring at him, he began to speak.

"We went down the stairs without a problem."

"Did you run or walk?"

"We walked quite slowly because Lydia appeared a little unsteady. Not drunk, or drugged, just a little out of it."

"She didn't stumble or fall?"

"No, nothing like that. She just walked very carefully. I took her to the library, and I stood by the hallway door. That one, nearest to the reception area. The other door was open. It leads out towards the dining room. But no one came in or went out. I'm absolutely certain of that."

"What about Lydia?"

"She went up to that row of books to the right of the fireplace and scanned them. She was looking for a book to read. I sat down on the sofa where the coffee table is lying and waited. She may have taken a biscuit. I didn't watch every move she made. I was looking around the room myself."

"What about the drink?"

"I know there was some liquid in the cup because she came across to me, white as a sheet, and fainted. Just where you saw us. I gave her a sip of the liquid. It looked like water. I'm sure it was water. Then she convulsed and spilt the cup and bottle and the coffee table crashed over as well. That's when you came in."

Ella and Frank sat in silence. Elsie was busy scribbling in her notebook and Alf looked as if all the troubles of the world has just tumbled multitudinously onto his shoulders. "I've let her be poisoned, haven't I?"

"What about the tea upstairs in her room?" pondered Frank.

"Yes," said Ella. "You said she seemed to be a bit unsteady on her feet as she came downstairs?"

"She was."

Elsie looked up from her note-taking. "PC Hydon, go upstairs and retrieve a sample for testing. Close the door behind you."

PC Hydon leapt to his feet and exited the library by the hallway door, glad to be away from the scene of the crime.

Ella got up and wandered around the library. Apart from the coffee table and the spilt contents, everything seemed to be in its place. She stopped by the other door. On the carpet was a card.

"Oh, my word, another card" she exclaimed. She leant forward to pick it up but Elsie, Sergeant Knowle, shouted. "Don't touch it!" She came quickly around the table putting on some plastic gloves and carefully placed the card in another transparent evidence bag.

"Do you ever run out of those?" asked Frank pointing at the bag.

"Thankfully no. I always keep a good supply of them. Just as well, eh?"

Sergeant Knowle placed the bag on the table. They could all clearly see the writing on the card. As before, the text was typewritten and contained some lyrics.

*"Who broke my heart, you did, you did*
*Bow to the target, blame Cupid*
*You think you're smart, that's stupid*
*Right from the start when you knew we would part*
*Shoot that poison arrow to my heart*
*Shoot that poison arrow."*

Frank read it out. "Do you know your ABC?" he asked cryptically.

"Here comes the schoolmaster in him again!" replied Ella.

"No, ABC, Martin Fry, the Sheffield group from the 1980s."

"The Look of Love?"

"That's the group, Sergeant Knowle," said Frank with a twinkle in his eyes. "Poison Arrow was one of their biggest hits."

"So according to the card," suggested Sergeant Knowle, "Lydia was poisoned with an arrow to the heart?"

"If she's dead," countered Ella.

"I didn't see any arrow. If she is dead then it's likely she was poisoned by the tea, the drink or the biscuit."

"What about a tiny arrow, like an arrow from a blow dart?"

"This card is putting ideas in our heads that..." began Ella.

"May not even be true," finished Frank.

"Someone's playing games with us. Deadly games. And at the moment, they're winning."

PC Hydon dashed upstairs to find the door to Lydia's bedroom locked. He plodded downstairs to the Reception and rang the bell. After what seemed an eternity to him, Martha appeared from the hotel office door.

"I can't get into Lydia Spooner's bedroom," he gasped.

"Pardon. Why would you....?"

"Never mind that. In the name of the law, I need to retrieve an important piece of evidence from her bedroom."

"OK, I'll get the pass keycard. Wait here, please."

"Hurry up!"

Martha moved a little quicker and returned holding the key card. She led the way at double-time up the stairs to the room. She unlocked the door and PC Hydon bustled past her. Looking around the room, he couldn't see any refreshments at all.

"Where's the tea things? They were there on the table."

"Oh those. I was told to go and clear them away."

"Who by?"

"Reeves, of course. It's normal practice. Go back after about half an hour and take away the tea or coffee trays."

"But, they was evidence!" PC Hydon couldn't believe his luck.

"I'm sorry. I wasn't to know. I knocked on the door. It was open so I went in and retrieved the tea tray. Same as I always do. I've done it a hundred times."

"Yes, all right. Where is the tray now?"

"Downstairs in the kitchen. I put it in the washer. Like I always do."

"You've destroyed the evidence!"

"I wasn't to know." Martha looked ready to burst into tears.

PC Hydon looked around in blustering frustration.

"Why was the door locked just now?"

"I always close the door behind me. Most people take their keycards with them. I'm always told to leave the place tidy. So, I always close the doors behind me. You can't be too careful. There may be thieves about!"

"Thank you. I'd better go and report this to my sergeant. She's not going to be very pleased!"

Martha gave a well-practised look around the room and shuffled towards the door. PC Hydon took the hint and made his way out of the room and started to go downstairs. Martha closed the door behind her and pushed it to ensure it was securely shut.

As PC Hydon started to go back to the library, his walkie talkie buzzed. He stopped at the top of the stairs, allowing Martha to continue on her back to the staff office.

"Yes, hello, PC Hydon here."

He listened to the message said, "Oh no!"

The messenger continued for a few moments more.

PC Hydon grunted "Thank you" and replaced his walkie talkie onto his uniform.

"It's the chop for you, Alf Hydon!" he grunted to himself as he began to descend the stairs on the way to his execution.

PC Hydon knocked and entered the library. Ella, Frank and Elsie looked up as he stood there, shuffling from foot to foot.

"Yes, PC Hydon? Bad news?"

"'Fraid so, ma'am. Dreadful news. I suppose you want my resignation?"

"Why ever for? We both take responsibility for anything that happens here."

Ella turned towards Alf.

"She's dead, isn't she?"

"Yes, Mrs. Raleigh. Poisoned. She died on the way to

154

Axminster Hospital."

Ella burst into tears. "That's awful. We're in the middle of a nightmare and it keeps getting worse."

Frank stood up. "No, now it's time to wake up from this nightmare. We've got a serial killer in our midst and the list of suspects is getting shorter by the day."

Elsie nodded. "Let's get all the guests and staff that we've got left together here in the library and let them know what's happened." She turned to Ella. "I'll do the talking. Your job is to watch for reactions."

"And Frank and I will stay by each of the doors just in case someone tries to escape," added PC Hydon.

"With a bit of luck, our murderer will give themselves away and we'll get this whole sorry episode sorted for once and for all!"

# CHAPTER 16

# JUMP

Martha and Reeves went around to all of the rooms in the hotel and told everyone they met to go immediately to the library. Sergeant Knowle had gone to Cornelius' room to break the latest news to him in private.

Fifteen minutes later everyone was gathered. Reeves had brought in extra seats enabling everyone to be seated.

There was Cornelius, Imelda Spooner the sixth wife, Albert Hamm the drummer, Johnny Toogood the guitarist, Davy "Lazybones" Bartholomew the double bassist, Ronnie "Fingers" Ryan the pianist, Emanuel the chef, Reeves the butler and Martha the receptionist and waitress. Alf, PC Hydon, stood by one door and Frank by another. Elsie, Sergeant Knowle stood in the middle of the room by the mahogany table. Ella sat with her back to the bookshelf on the right hand of the fireplace.

"Right, is everybody here?" asked Sergeant Knowle.

Everyone looked around and nodded.

"Now, I'm afraid I've got some further bad news for you," began Sergeant Knowle.

"It's Lydia, isn't it?" shouted Imelda. "She's been murdered. Just like all the rest. Hasn't she?"

"Well, it's not the way I would have announced it, but yes. You're correct. Lydia Spooner appears to have been poisoned. Unless someone can prove otherwise, I can only surmise that the murderer is in this room!"

Everyone gasped in astonishment. There were mutterings of "No!" and "That's not possible!"

Ronnie "Fingers" Ryan raised a hand. Sergeant Knowle nodded.

"Excuse me, but who would want to kill her? She'd only been here a little while. I speak for everybody in the band when I say that we had never even met her. Cornelius never brought her to any of the gigs I played. What about you, Albert?"

"You're absolutely right. I never met her."

Both of the other two band members nodded in agreement.

"Thank you for that. I'm going to have to ask every one of you exactly where you were this afternoon since lunch."

Cornelius, the band and Imelda immediately answered. "In our own rooms with the door locked."

Emanuel had been in the kitchen. Martha in either the office or at reception. Reeves had been in the staff office and preparing the dining room for the evening meal.

"Has anyone got anything they'd like to say?" asked Sergeant Knowle.

"Yes," said Cornelius, getting to his feet. "I'd like to go home. Stuff the rest of the tour. This break has almost broken me. I want to leave this wretched hotel and go home."

"Well, I'm sorry, extremely sorry," replied Sergeant

Knowle, "but that's just not possible."

"Why not?"

"Because you're a suspect in a murder enquiry. No-one will be leaving this place until we've apprehended the murderer."

"And when will that be?" Cornelius temper was steadily rising to the surface.

Frank coughed and took a step forward. "Tomorrow, Mr. Spooner. Tomorrow, everyone in this room will be free to leave. Except for the murderer."

The evening meal was another sombre affair. Imelda Spooner had her meal in her room. Ella offered to eat with her, but the offer was politely rejected. The band members sat together and immediately after the meal went out for a ramble around the grounds to take in what was left of the evening sun.

Cornelius returned to his room. PC Hydon patrolled the corridor between Imelda and Cornelius' room.

Ella and Frank returned to their room intending to go through Alice's research. Frank picked up his bag and began to open it. "Where's the other bag?"

Ella sat in her chair with a nonplussed look on her face.

"I don't know."

"Didn't you bring it back to the room?"

"No, I carried it around with me. I thought I'd be able to just pop it in here, but things happened."

"When did you last have it?"

Ella thought hard. Then she clapped her hands in delighted recognition.

"Lydia's room. I put it down in Lydia's room. By the tea

tray."

"Well, you'd better get someone to let you into the room so you can retrieve it. You do that and I'll start to go through this bag."

Frank looked through the bag in his possession. Ella was correct. There was lots of information about each of the wives.

Diane, Cornelius' first true love. Divorced quietly with no fuss. She seemed a bit of a dreamer. Probably still in love. Betty the non-swimmer again divorced quietly with no fuss.

Jane. Jane? Alice could find out little about her. Married and divorced in quite a quick succession.

Lydia. Now, she was feisty. Her divorce took a long time to sort out. Must have cost Cornelius even more money. No wonder he had to keep on the road. He needed money the way the rest of us need bread and water. He still needs money. Now if he got rid of all of them then his outgoings would be drastically reduced.

Imelda was married for five years and only divorced last year.

Who's number six? Alice doesn't mention anything about her. Perhaps Ella's bag will have more to say about her.

Ella returned to their room looking confused and a little brow-beaten.

"What's the problem?"

"It's the bag. I eventually found Martha and she let me in to Lydia's room. But the bag isn't there. Martha convinced it wasn't there when she cleared up the tea things. Someone's taken it."

"Well, the room was empty when you and Elsie followed

Alf downstairs to see Lydia."

"Yes, we left the door open. I'm quite sure of that."

"So anybody could have popped in and helped themselves?"

"Yes." Ella sat down on the bed. "Sorry, I should have kept the bag with me."

"Don't worry. I've been through the contents of my bag and there's nothing really there that we didn't know already," comforted Frank.

"Like what?"

"Details of the wives and their divorces. Cornelius is going to be saving himself a lot of money! He's down to two now!"

"Imelda and wife number six. Who is she?"

"I don't know," responded Frank quizzically, "I was hoping your bag would tell me about that."

"We'll need to talk to Alice again." Ella yawned.

Frank smiled. "It's been a long day. Let's sort it out in the morning. Things always look clearer after a good night's sleep."

Despite all the terrible goings-on at the Cobb Country House Hotel, the standard of catering remained top-notch. Breakfast the next morning kept up the high standard. Guests had no complaints about the food. They all assembled as the gong rang. Apart from Imelda, it was a full house.

Immediately after breakfast, Cornelius turned to Sergeant Knowle and demanded: "When are you going to solve these murders. You promised we could leave today."

"All in good time, Mr. Spooner." Elsie smiled and turning

her back on him, walked away.

"Hey, you can't just ignore me!"

Elsie stopped and looking over her shoulder remarked. "I don't think anybody could ever ignore you, Mr. Spooner. Have a good morning."

*Aargh, stir it in.*

*Always good to start the day with a cuppa.*

*Gloves on?*

*Calling card at the ready?*

*Don't worry, little lady. Just follow the watch.*

*You're feeling sleepy.*

*But still, you're going for a little walk.*

*Find a place where you can fly?*

*And then just fly away.*

*You won't feel a thing. Well, not much anyway.*

*One small step, little lady, and … Jump.*

*Don't you just love how lightweight they are?*

*Sweet dreams.*

*Drum roll, please.*

Ella and Frank were talking together in the library when Martha appeared.

"Sorry to bother you, but I can't find Mrs. Spooner."

"Imelda?" asked Ella.

"Yes, I carried her tea up to her. Reeves was going to do it but he was needed for breakfast, so I took it. She was dressed but she didn't look, er, totally with it."

"Interesting."

"I went up half an hour later to serve her breakfast and she wasn't there. She'd had some tea, only about half a cup. Her coat had gone from the back of her door and, I think, she was wearing some outdoors shoes. There was a little dried mud on the carpet."

"You've searched the grounds?"

"Yes, I did a quick scoot around."

"There's no way she would have got past the special constable on the back gate. I'd better go and check just in case," responded Ella with determination. She made to leave the room.

"There *is* another way out that is quite secret," muttered Martha almost to herself. "Not even the staff know about it. Us village children know but…"

Ella stopped and turned back towards Martha. "Where is it?"

"Behind the archery range, there's a small hole in the hedge and fence. The hedge is pretty deep. It catches any arrows that stray wide of the target. She could have got out that way. In fact, it wouldn't surprise me if she did."

"Why?"

"Well, I'm pretty sure I saw her come back that way from her walk the other day."

Ella turned to Frank, "Where would she go? She must realise she's in danger."

Martha appeared thoughtful as she slowly offered another piece of information. "I think I may be able to help with that as well."

"How? Tell us," urged Frank.

"The other day she asked me about local walks, and I told her about Cannington Viaduct. She said it sounds perfect."

"Yes, we met her or *thought* we met her," said Ella.

"She was on the other end of the viaduct. I think we disturbed her from something."

Martha gasped. "You don't think she was planning to jump, do you?"

"Oh, my word!" stuttered Ella.

"You may be right. And after all the terrible things that have happened here in the past few days, she may have literally been tipped over the edge."

"We need to get there immediately."

"You'll never catch her up by walking," said Martha. "Use your car. Take the A3052 towards Lyme Regis for about two miles and then turn left down into Cannington Lane. The viaduct's about half a mile along that road!"

Frank nodded "Thanks!"

Ella took control. "Grab what you need, Frank, and meet me at the car!"

Two miles along the road, they turned left into a narrow hardly used lane. Half a mile later the viaduct loomed up in front of them. They parked on the grass verge beside a whitewashed house.

"We need a plan of action," Frank began.

"Yes, I'm going up that path over there!" Ella pointed towards the far end of the viaduct. "You head for the other end."

Frank could see a gate leading into a field underneath the viaduct. "I'll find a way around the trees and up to that path we used the other day."

"When you're up there be nice and gentle. No shouting. If she's near the edge, I'll distract her so you can get as close to her as possible. Don't put yourself in danger but grab her if you can."

"No problem. See you in a bit. Love you!"

"I love you too. Very much! Don't take any risks!"

Frank ran along the lane towards the viaduct, climbed over the gate and made his way up towards the viaduct. Ella headed through the gate by the house and climbed steadily towards the far end of the viaduct.

Martha found Sergeant Knowle and told her what had happened and where Ella and Frank had gone.

"Ah, rats! I can't spare anybody from the hotel. We'll just have to leave it up to them. They'll phone me if they need any backup."

PC Hydon approached the pair. "Ma'am, there's a lady at the front gates who wants to come in. Says her name is Annie Saxon, Cornelius' number one fan."

"I hope you told her 'No'!"

"Yes, ma'am, but she is very insistent. Says it's a matter of life and death."

"Right. I'll go and talk to her when I get word from Frank and Ella."

"Why?"

"Imelda Spooner has disappeared, and they think she's heading for the Cannington Viaduct."

"That's a death trap!" PC Hydon looked alarmed.

"I know. I'm thinking that wife number five may not need help from our murderer."

"For once, we could have done with your sticky tracker."

"Shall I go and get it from the car?"

"No, PC Hydon, it's a bit late for it now."

PC Hydon stood ruminating.

"You think she'll jump?"

Martha and Sergeant Knowle both nodded.

"Is there anybody else missing?" asked PC Hydon.

"My word! I never thought... Alf, check them all. They were all there at breakfast but..."

"On my way, ma'am!"

Frank and Ella took fifteen strenuous minutes to reach each end of the viaduct and it was obvious to both of them that their educated guesswork was correct. There in the middle of the viaduct was Imelda. She was sat down amongst the weeds and scrub bushes. She appeared to be staring at the north wall of the viaduct. Frank kept to the south wall and crouching made his way towards her, using the bushes as a far from adequate form of cover. He could see Ella at the other end of the bridge following his example.

They both tried to stay out of sight for as long as possible. Frank was lucky and got to within fifteen yards of Imelda before she started to sense she was now not alone. At that moment, Ella spoke.

"Hello, Mrs. Spooner. Fancy seeing you here again."

Imelda turned toward Ella and Frank took the opportunity to move closer.

"Oh hi. I know you, don't I?"

"Yes, Mrs. Spooner or can I call you Imelda?"

"Er, yes, call me anything you want. It doesn't matter now."

"Why, is something wrong?"

"Oh, everything. I feel so useless, so weary. I'm tired of it all."

"Is that why you're sitting here? Trying to get away from it all?"

"I think so. I'm not sure." Imelda paused and stood up.

"Perhaps it's time to see."

"To see what?" Ella was trying desperately hard to keep her voice calm and under control.

Imelda turned towards the viaduct wall and moved swiftly towards the edge.

"To see if I can fly!"

She launched herself upwards and over at exactly the same time as Frank propelled himself in a pretty good impression of a rugby tackle.

# CHAPTER 17

# THREE STEPS TO HEAVEN

Frank made two phone calls. The first one was a 999 call to the ambulance service. The ambulance soon arrived in Cannington Road near their car. Two paramedics carefully but firmly escorted Imelda down from the viaduct and into the ambulance.

"I'm going with her," said Ella. "She needs a friend until she's settled into the hospital."

"Absolutely," replied Frank.

The paramedics dared not disagree.

The second phone call was to Sergeant Knowle to update her on their eventful morning.

When Frank arrived back at the hotel, he went straight up to their room to change out of his torn and dirty trousers.

Lying on one of the pillows on their bed was a card. He could see the front contained the words "Best Wishes, Cornelius."

Turning it over by the edges, Frank read the words:

*Might as well jump*
*Might as well jump*

*Go ahead and jump*
*Go ahead and jump*
*Ow, oh, hey, you*
*Who said that?*
*Baby, how you been?*
*You say you don't know*
*You won't know until you begin.*

Frank stared at the words *Go ahead and jump. Might as well jump*. It was some sort of command. Not exactly the most eloquent of lyrics.

His thoughts were disturbed by the sound of an ambulance siren outside on the main road. Frank quickly changed in a clean pair of jeans, washed his grubby hands and scuffed knees. When he was ready, he once again held the card by its edges and rushed off to find Sergeant Knowle.

She was with PC Hydon standing outside the hotel entrance surveying the crowds beyond the gates. The skies had been clear blue for the last couple of days but now banks of dark clouds were visible in the western sky.

"I think there be more 'ere today than yesterday," offered PC Hydon.

"Yes, but for how much longer? Looks like rain's on its way." Sergeant Knowles indicated the looming clouds.

"That'll soon frighten them all away."

Frank stood alongside the weather forecasters.

"Hello, Frank. Excellent work, by the way."

"Any time you want a game for our police rugby team, you let me know!" laughed PC Hydon.

"I found this on our bed. I avoided any fingerprints."

"PC Hydon, evidence bag, please."

Alf immediately produced one and Frank slipped it inside. Both Sergeant Knowle and PC Hydon took their time reading the message.

"It's not from any song I know," said Frank.

"That be Van Halen. With that guitarist who died."

"Jump. By Van Halen," echoed Sergeant Knowle.

Frank voiced his thoughts. "Go ahead and jump? You know, if I didn't know any better, I'd say she was hypnotised or drugged."

"Did she act that way?"

"Yes, definitely. She was just sitting on the bridge staring at the viaduct walls. Martha noticed her manner earlier as well." Frank stopped. "Any news from Ella?"

"They took Imelda to Axminster Hospital. I sent a police car to bring Ella straight back here as soon as she's happy to let the hospital staff take care of Imelda."

Frank spoke with some hesitance. "I think I know who's behind all this."

"Really?" PC Hydon was all ears. "Who?"

"No, wait a while. I need to get my thoughts together."

"Are we getting all *Poirot* and *Death in Paradise* again?" PC Hydon rubbed his hands together in glee. "Mind you, it'll be good to get this one over."

Sergeant Knowle faced Frank. "Can you be sure you know who the murderer is?"

"Almost!"

"Well, I'll be glad to sort this out as well. The Assistant Chief Constable is finally sending us Inspector Wilkins. He'll be here this afternoon to take over the case."

"A lot of good he'll be," whispered PC Hydon.

"Alf! A bit of respect for a senior officer!"

"Sorry, ma'am. You know what I mean."

"Yes, but if Frank has got it right, then we won't need the Inspector," smiled Sergeant Knowle.

Frank held up a hand. "Let's wait until Ella gets back from the hospital. Until then, I suggest we tell no one about this morning's episode. No one, OK? Let's keep all our guests in their rooms. For their own safety!"

Ella arrived back from Axminster in time for lunch. Frank and Ella sat alone in the dining room. They shared their thoughts about the events of the morning. Everyone else took their meals in their rooms. Martha was rushing up and down stairs all through the meal but still made time to serve them.

Ella listened to Frank and nodded. "I think you're right. But it's another thing to prove it."

"Well, on our previous occasions, the guilty party have given themselves away."

"One way or another!"

The four of them, Frank, Ella, Elsie and Alf met in the library after lunch. Ella spoke to Reeves as they were leaving the dining room. "We'll be in the library and are not to be disturbed under any circumstances."

Reeves tapped his foot but replied, "Yes, ma'am."

Frank closed both doors and they sat around the mahogany table on the mahogany chairs.

"How is Imelda?" asked Elsie.

"Drugged but alive. I'm convinced our murderer was aiming to kill wife number five."

"But he or she didn't succeed, did they?" said Elsie.

"Thanks to Frank," rooted Alf.

"Down to business." Elsie attempted to bring the meeting

to order. "Frank, you said this morning, you had a good idea who our murderer was?"

"Yes, indeed. But first of all, I need to find out a few things."

"Tell us," said Elsie, "and I'll put Alf onto it at once."

"No," said Frank, "it's not information as such."

The three waited for him to explain.

"I need to know about three talents. Number one - who is a good drummer? Two - who has good archery skills? And three - who is practised in the art of toxicology?"

Ella understood what Frank meant. "Our murderer will have talents in all three areas."

Frank continued. "I know about the first and the third talents. It's the archery that intrigues me!"

"Wait a minute," said Ella. "Wasn't there someone using a crossbow the other day?"

"Of course," shouted Frank. "That's it. Sorted."

Frank stood up and addressed the meeting.

"Ladies and gentleman, I know who the murderer is."

"Who?" asked Alf.

"Gather the occupants of the Cobb Country House Hotel together and I'll let you know!"

# CHAPTER 18

# WHAT'S GOING ON

Frank and Ella made their way upstairs to prepare for the meeting. As they reached their bedroom, they found Annie Saxon sitting outside their door.

"What are you doing here?" asked Frank.

Annie smiled.

"How did you get past the policemen on duty?"

"Ask me no secrets and I'll tell you no lies." Annie continued smiling.

"There are no dustbins up here!"

"No, it's not dustbins I'm looking for, but you. There's a few things you should know."

"Well, come in," said Ella. She waved Annie into the room.

Annie sat down in the chair by the window, leaving Ella and Frank perched on their comfortable, hand crafted bed.

"You do know we're about to confront our murderer, don't you?" said Ella.

"Oh good. Then I'm just in time."

"Let me guess what you're going to tell us," continued Ella.

"Go on, have a go but you'll never guess."

"Annie Saxon or should I say, Annie Spooner. You're wife number six. You're married to Cornelius Spooner!"

Annie laughed out loud. "Wow. I didn't expect that! Well done. How did you know?"

"The rings," said Frank. "You're wearing Yin and Yang Wedding Rings. His is gold and yours is white gold. He's got that comma symbol and so have you. I noticed yours when we first met you and Ella saw the matching ring on Cornelius."

"Yes, Cornelius will insist on wearing all his rings and they're all gold. They must be worth a lot but he won't sell a single one of them."

"What's the other thing you were going to tell us?"

"I recognised someone from the past the other day outside the gates. It took me a while to trawl through the memories, but I eventually went up to her and introduced myself."

"Alice Aylesbeare?"

"Yes, yet again, how did you know? I hadn't seen her for years. You're very good!"

"She's a friend of ours. And also, the secretary of the Cornelius Spooner fan club- The CIA, I believe, it's called?"

"Exactly. She invited me home for the night. My B&B was only for a night. I've been living rough for a few days."

"You were searching for food in the dustbins?"

"Well, sort of."

Frank continued. "And Alice told you about the

drummer?"

"Yes. Am I telling you or are you telling me?" Annie looked a little deflated.

"Sorry. We'll keep quiet. You tell us the story."

"Cornelius is not perfect, heaven knows. And in his younger days, he stole a song from his drummer. *The Night is Still Young*. It was his biggest hit and it made him a fortune. His name is on the publishing credits. But he never wrote a note of it."

Both Frank and Ella nodded but said nothing.

"And the writer of that song is here in this hotel at this very moment and...."

There was a knock on the door and PC Hydon barged in. "It's all set up. We're all downstairs. I've set up the chairs in the library just the way you had them in Sidmouth. Are you ready?"

"Well, yes." Frank and Ella wanted to carry on with Annie's story.

"Well, come on then. Is she coming with you? Is she part of your great 'de-now-mount' as the French say?"

"Yes, Alf, she is. We're on our way."

Ella, Frank and Annie got up and headed out of the room following in the gigantic footsteps of PC Alf Hydon.

The four of them entered the library to be met by an expectant audience spread around the room. Sergeant Knowle was standing by the far door. PC Hydon having opened the hallway door for the other three, remained to guard that door.

All eyes locked onto Frank and Ella except Cornelius whose eyes were fixed uncomprehendingly on Annie.

Frank looked around the room.

Besides Cornelius, seated in a comfy old armchair by the fire, there were the four members of the Portobello Crooners, drummer Albert Hamm, double bassist Dave "Lazybones" Bartholomew, pianist Ronnie "Fingers" Ryan and guitarist Johnny Toogood. They too were seated in the comfy armchairs. Martha the waitress, Emanuel the chef and Reeves the butler all sat on the mahogany chairs around the mahogany library table. Annie Saxon joined them on a spare chair.

The fire had been lit due to the colder weather. Outside, the rain was falling steadily. In the library, the room was electric.

"Good afternoon, everybody," began Sergeant Knowle. "You all know why you're here. There are thirteen of us in this room and one of us..." She paused for dramatic effect. "is a serial murderer."

She waited for the effect to sink in and then continued. "Frank and Ella Raleigh have been assisting us in our enquiries and between the four of us..." she nodded at PC Hydon who stood like a statue by the hallway door, "we have come to our conclusions."

Frank took up the narrative. "We thought you may appreciate the results of our deliberations."

Cornelius shrugged his shoulders. "Just tell us, mate!"

"All in good time," Ella responded.

"First," continued Frank, "Some background story."

Ella advanced the narrative. "A long time ago there was a famous pop star living in London looking for his big break. Sure, he had some hits, but he was looking for that career-defining song. Then, one day, just as he was walking into rehearsals with his band, he heard *The Night is Still Young*. The band were playing it. He immediately recognised its hit potential. This was it? He would be able to sing it bigger and better than any other singer in London. It was as if it had been written for Cornelius Spooner."

Frank took over. "The song was indeed written just for him. When he went into the room, the band played it for him. He fell in love with it. A week later they were in a tiny recording studio somewhere in Soho. A month later it was released, and they had themselves their biggest hit."

Alice Aylesbeare and her bags had filled them in with the background details.

"Carry on, Ella."

"Thank-you. There is, however, one problem that has reverberated down the years. When the record came out, the label stated that the song was written by Cornelius Spooner. In fact, the song was, as far as we know, written by the drummer in the band. That drummer never received one penny in royalties."

"Scandalous," muttered Albert Hamm.

"Indeed," answered Frank. "Well, you all know the Portobello Crooners. The personnel were forever changing..."

"Evolving," stated Cornelius.

"And," continued Frank, "the drummer was soon gone to pastures new, a footnote in the band's history."

Martha put up her hand. "I don't understand what this has to do with all these terrible deaths?"

"Sorry, Martha my dear," answered Ella with a twinkle in her eye.

The six musicians in the room smirked in recognition.

Frank saw the smirk and internally sighed in relief. He was on the right track!

"Right," interrupted Sergeant Knowle. "My turn to fill you in on a few facts now." Everyone swivelled their gaze to the far door.

"All the murders *could* have been accidents. They were all planned to appear that way. The first one, Diane Streamer, could have slipped on the wet gravel and fallen down the well. She didn't. She was pushed. She was murdered."

Strangely, Elsie was beginning to enjoy her performance.

"Stop it," she thought, "you're a policewoman. This is serious." She resumed her narrative.

"The second murder of Betty Brook-Spooner, down at the Cobb, could have been an accidental drowning. It wasn't. It, too, was murder."

Every eye in the room was focused on Elsie as she continued.

"The third murder, when Jane Spooner was shot by the archery arrow, could have been another tragic accident. It wasn't. It was murder. Perpetrated by the archery expert in this room."

Johnny Toogood gasped and tore his eyes away from Elsie. He stared across the room at the archery expert.

"The fourth murder happened in this very room." Martha moaned in disgust. "It could have been an accident, but, of all of the incidents, this one was undoubtedly murder. Four murders committed by one person. All four victims were former wives of Cornelius Spooner."

There was a collective gasp around the room except for Emanuel who was struggling to understand and follow the implications of the policewomen's words and Reeves who sat there impassively.

Elsie waited and continued. "The murderer may have got

away with the first three murders if they hadn't been a bit too clever. They left behind a card with each murder giving us some significant clues. Each card had some form of a song lyric or rhyme on one side. And on the other 'Best Wishes. Cornelius'."

Elsie nodded at Frank. He continued.

"At first, we thought that was all the proof we needed to pin the murders on Cornelius. He didn't have an alibi for any of the murders. There was no doubt, he had the opportunity to murder each of his wives. But a tiny mark on the cards changed my mind. Between the 'Best wishes' and the name 'Cornelius' was a full stop, not a comma. The card could have been a mocking comment aimed at Cornelius, not written by Cornelius. It could have been the murderer offering a mocking best wishes about the death of an ex-wife."

Ella took up the tale. "We asked ourselves some questions. Was Cornelius that desperate to cut back on his outgoings that he was willing to knock off his ex-wives one by one? Was wife number six obsessed with jealousy? Did someone have a grudge against the wives? Or against Cornelius? Did the drummer, the writer of Cornelius' biggest hit, want to take some deadly revenge?"

Frank clapped his hands and drew everyone's attention to him. "I think we've wasted enough of your time. Let me finish but telling you who our murderer is."

All eyes swivelled from Elsie back to Frank.

"The murderer has three talents. First. They are a superb drummer."

"That's you out, Albert Hamm," chortled Cornelius.

"Shut up, Cornie," snapped Albert. "This is serious."

"Their second talent is they have to be an archery expert.

The shot that killed Jane was the shot of an expert."

Johnny Toogood made to stand up, "Then I…"

Frank held up his hand. "I'd prefer a confession first - not an accusation."

Johnny understood and then sat down.

"And thirdly they have to have an interest in toxicology - the art of poison…."

Martha gasped again. "That book. On the counter. It was…"

Frank raised a finger to his lips. "Wait, Martha!"

"Now, has anyone got anything to say? Is the murderer in the room willing to stand up and confess?"

No-one moved.

"If there is not a confession, then, I think, we'll move onto the extra information that will undoubtedly convict our murderer."

Reeves coughed. "Excuse me Mr. Raleigh, but haven't you forgotten the fifth wife?"

"No," interrupted Sergeant Knowle, "I didn't need to mention her. Because she is still alive."

"I thought she jumped off Cannington Viaduct?"

"Really, how did you come by that information? It's confidential."

Reeves was stunned.

"She tried to jump," added Ella, "but my husband saved her. She's safely tucked up in Axminster Hospital. They tell us she was drugged."

"We believe the drug was in the tea that Martha brought up to Imelda this morning," Frank added.

"I didn't make the tea," stuttered Martha.

"No, we guessed as such."

"The only people who could have made the tea were Emanuel and Reeves."

"'Eeeee make the tea," shouted Emanuel. "Eeee always make it!!!!"

"Now wait a moment." Reeves drummed his hands on the table in front of him.

"And Reeves is my archery expert. But I expect you already knew that!" shouted Johnny Toogood. Frank nodded.

"And that book on the counter about poisons. It's his book," screamed Martha, pointing along the table at Reeves.

Reeves stood up. He removed two kitchen knives from the inside pockets of his jacket. He began drumming them on the table in front of him. "Ladies and gentlemen, if you think that I am the sort of person who would seek revenge on that guttersnipe Spooner for stealing my song and taking millions of pounds in royalties that were rightfully mine... If you think that I would be the sort of person who would take great enjoyment in seeing a faded and over-the-hill warbler like Spooner suffer whilst one by one, I eliminated his precious wives, then...."

Reeves had been all the time edging around the table towards the hallway door. He headed at an alarming speed for Alf Hydon swirling the knives in front of him. He crashed through the door. Alf managed to slap him on the back but was unable to do anything to stop him.

"...then you're right!!!" Reeves screamed as he headed for the front door of the hotel.

# CHAPTER 19

## RUNAWAY

The library occupants were stunned.

"That little rat!" shouted Cornelius. "Are you going to let him get away?"

"After him, PC Hydon!" shouted Sergeant Knowle as she exited through the far door.

PC Hydon turned and walked through the hallway door and headed for the front door.

The rain was now teeming down causing mini explosions as it splattered on the hotel entrance paving. Reeves was already at the front gates waving his knives around his head. What few police, journalists, villagers and other onlookers were left standing in the pouring rain hastily moved aside. One policewoman tried to block the gates. Reeves screamed "I'll stab you!" and she moved rapidly out of harm's way.

As PC Hydon reached the gates, Reeves had crossed the main road and was splashing down a narrow country lane opposite the Cobb Country House Hotel.

Sergeant Knowle caught Alf up. She had donned wet

weather gear and as they stopped to safely cross the road asked: "Can't you go any quicker, Alf?"

"Oi'm saving myself, ma'am. Gonna be a long haul." He stopped, pulled his police hat further down over his head and put his hands on his hips. "In fact, why am Oi bothering? We got a car back at the hotel. Let's use that."

"No, you use that. Check out the local map and see if you can get ahead of him and cut him off. I'll keep in pursuit."

At that moment Ella arrived in their car with Frank in the passenger seat. "Bit wet out. Do you want a lift, Sergeant Knowle?" Ella asked with a twinkle in her eye.

Johnny Toogood and Martha arrived with raised umbrellas beside the car. "Where is he? Which way did he go?" Johnny was all too willing to give pursuit and apprehend the murderous butler.

"I can't believe I worked with him and he was such a...." Martha struggled to find the right words.

"Whatever you're going to say, I agree," said Johnny.

"Enough of this talk. We need action!" Sergeant Knowle resumed command. "Johnny and Martha. You carry on down this lane. BUT... You are not to go anywhere near him. Stay under cover and just keep Reeves under observation. I'm going to head across the fields in this direction. She pointed towards Lyme Regis. Frank and Ella, you take the car and head along the main road towards Seaton and take the next left and come parallel to this lane. If he goes to the west, you let us all know. If he's gone east, I'll let you all know."

"Before we go, have we all got mobile phones?" asked Frank.

Everyone nodded. "Right, here's my number." Frank read out the number and Johnny, Martha and Elsie tapped it soggily into their phones. "Phone me whenever you have any information and I'll share it around. If you haven't got any information, then phone me every fifteen minutes for my update."

"Good idea," said Sergeant Knowle. "Don't do anything stupid. Let's be careful out there. He's killed at least four people. I forbid you to give him a reason to kill any more!"

Martha smiled.

"I mean it. This is serious. Don't take any chances!"

Everyone nodded in agreement and set off.

Johnny and Martha began running down the lane avoiding the streams and puddles of water that were traversing the roadway. Ella backed the car to the main road. Elsie found a farm gate and made her way diagonally across the grassy field towards a line of trees.

PC Hydon splashed his way back to their police car parked in the hotel car park. He picked up a bag lying on the back seat and put it on the passenger seat in the front before driving off towards the front gate. There he briefly halted and told the policewoman on the gate to head into the hotel and make sure everyone was OK. "Make 'em a cup of tea or pour 'em some sort of drink. Calm 'em down. Get yourself some shelter from this pesky rain. Oi'll be downalong."

He checked the bag beside him and turned left towards Lyme Regis.

Frank fielded calls from the other three hunters but there were no sightings.

PC Hydon, unaware of the plan to communicate with Frank, phoned into Sergeant Knowle. "Oi'm in Ware

Lane. Lyme Regis. Oi'm undercover waiting by the South West Coast Path where it comes out of the Undercliff. If 'e be coming this way, oi'll nab 'im."

Twenty minutes later there was still no news.

PC Hydon again phoned in. "'E be headed this way, ma'am. Oi know it. Looks like tide's out so he may come along the beach. Whichever way 'e comes, oi've got 'im."

An hour later and still no news.

The rain appeared to be easing for a spell but there were plenty of dark clouds still stacked up in the west. Johnny and Martha had reached Stepps Road and were heading across the grounds of the Rousdon Estate aiming for the Coast Path.

Johnny was becoming impatient. He phoned Elsie directly. "Any sign of him?"

"No, you get to the Coast Path, find a good observation point and wait there," ordered Elsie.

"Will do!" replied Johnny.

Frank and Ella also phoned Elsie. "We've found a spot near Stepps Road. We can see clear along the coast as far as the visibility will allow. We're both pretty sure he hasn't got past us this way."

Frank had his phone on speaker-phone, so Ella joined in. "Frank's right. He's either holed up or headed east to Lyme Regis."

"Yes," agreed Elsie. "If I were on the run, I'd head for Lyme Regis and blend into the crowd. He wasn't dressed for a cold and rainy night out in the open."

Another thirty minutes went by without a sighting. Elsie had been pondering about whether she was following correct police procedure. She phoned PC Hydon.

"Alf, I think it's time we brought in more support. I'm going to phone Exeter and ask Inspector Wilkins for backup. If he says he's taking over, then I'm not going to argue."

"Wait ma'am. Oi know 'e's coming this way. Oi'd stake my life on it."

"I appreciate your confidence but if we've no sightings then we need more help."

There was a pause. A silence on the other end of the line. Then PC Alf Hydon whispered. "I've got 'im. I can see 'im. Through the mist. He's downalong the beach. Oi'm going after him."

"Great. Be careful. I'll head for the Cobb!"

Sergeant Knowle updated the other two groups on the sighting.

"Right," cried Ella. "We're on our way."

"Pick me up outside Peek House," exclaimed an excited Elsie. "If anyone stops you, tell them you're on police business."

"We'll be there in ten minutes or less!"

They were there in six minutes and were soon hurtling along the A3052 towards Lyme Regis.

PC Alf Hydon, carrying his bag, made his way along the South West Coast Path as it descended away from the Undercliff and into Lyme Regis. Now and again, he would stop, check inside the bag and then nodding his head, carry on.

Occasionally he lost sight of Reeves, but he knew exactly where they would rendezvous, and he set himself the task of a successful arrest. PC Hydon followed the Coast Path, through the wooden chalets, past the bowling green before walking briskly alongside the beach car park. Reeves was on Monmouth Beach heading towards the

Cobb.

PC Hydon reached the foot of Cobb Road before Reeves and parked himself under a shop awning and calmly awaited his arrival. He was pleased with his work so far and was determined and confident that he would complete the task he had set himself.

He could see Reeves stumbling along the beach, almost tripping over some of the larger pebbles. He looked completely sodden but was carrying his work jacket over one shoulder, his shirt sleeves were rolled up and as far as PC Hydon could see, he was no longer carrying the two kitchen knives.

"That'll make it easier!" PC Hydon whispered.

A child, also standing under the awning, was licking a strawberry ice cream. She turned to her mum and uttered in a loud voice. "…That policeman was talking to himself!"

"Go away," Alf almost begged.

"Mummy!!" yowled the child in an even louder voice, "He told me to go away. That's not very polite!!" The cry of the child rang loud and clear over the sound of the falling rain.

At that precise moment, Reeves appeared through the beach huts, no more than twenty yards away. Hearing the raucous wail of the child, he spotted PC Hydon, and abruptly changed direction. He headed away from Cobb Road and towards the Cobb itself.

Alf leapt out from under the awning. "Oi, you! Stop! You're wanted for murder!"

Those people scurrying between the raindrops beside the harbour stopped and seeing the object of PC Hydon's cry jumped back. A few women screamed and shouted. Reeves panicked and began running along the Cobb's lower walkway skidding on the slippery surface. PC Hydon stated the obvious. "You're trapped. There's no way out. He began chasing Reeves along the Cobb.

He was vaguely aware of a car blaring its horn followed by a cry of "Watch yourself, Alf Hydon."

The sound of Sergeant Knowle's voice strengthened his resolve. The cavalry had arrived!

Reeves had always appeared to be calm, cold and calculated around the hotel. That had all changed. He slithered, tottered and swerved along the Cobb.

PC Hydon waited for Sergeant Knowle. "'E ain't going nowhere fast."

"How were you so certain he would come this way?"

"I slapped one of my sticky trackers on 'is back as 'e dashed by me. It's still there!"

"Excellent. One of your gadgets that actually works!"

"Thank you, sarge."

"Right, let's get him."

The two of them carefully marched through the increasingly persistent rain, along the Cobb, towards their prey.

"If he runs towards you, get out of his way," muttered the Sergeant. "He may still be armed."

"I don't think 'e is, ma'am. There's no way 'e could 'ide those knives. 'E's soaked. 'Is shirt is see-through and his jacket is so floppy. No knives in there."

"I hope you're right. But take no chances."

They continued their march. Reeves made his way towards the end of the Cobb. He was now surrounded by the harbour water on one side and a turbulent sea on the other. Coming to his senses, he stopped and looked back. PC Hydon grimly smiled. "We've got 'im!"

Reeves carried on along the Cobb until all too quickly he reached the end. In front and on each side of him were the grey boisterous waves of Lyme Bay.

He stopped and climbed onto the upper walkway.

"That's stoopid!" PC Hydon murmured. "Only way is down." He climbed up to the Upper Walkway and stood twenty yards away with arms folded and a stoic expression on his face.

Sergeant Knowle moved swiftly along the lower walkway until she was level with Reeves.

"Reeves, it's over."

Reeves rotated his head to look at her.

"Let's get you inside somewhere out of the rain. You must be soaked. You'll catch your death of cold!"

"Shut up!" Reeves barked. "I'm not spending the rest of my life somewhere out of the rain. It's my money. Rightfully mine. He stole it from me. I wanted to make him suffer. The way I had to suffer. He ruined my life and now I've ruined his! I'm glad I did it."

Reeves turned his back on the Sergeant and as he did so, slipped off balance. His jacket was thrown into the air and landed with a clang at Sergeant Knowle's feet. With a smothered cry, Reeves grasped at thin air and stumbled, almost in slow motion, off the walkway and into the unforgiving turbulent waters of Lyme Bay.

Sergeant Knowles and PC Hydon rushed to the spot where he had fallen in.

"No, you are not to dive in there and save him. It's too dangerous."

"I wasn't going to, ma'am. I'm not that stoopid!"

The two of them stood watching the spot where he had

fallen in. Nothing appeared on the surface. No body, nothing.

Elsie picked up the jacket with the kitchen knives clashing in the deep inside pocket. Alf stared at them in astonishment.

"'E's gone. Just like that."

# CHAPTER 20

# NEVER EVEN SAID GOODBYE

It was late in the evening when Sergeant Knowle and PC Hydon reported to Inspector Wilkins in the old police station in Hill Road. They explained all that had happened during that day.

Inspector Wilkins listened, "Well, that seems all very straight forward. However, I will need to refer your behaviour to my superiors in Exeter. You should have made some attempt to save the poor man."

Alf's face looked fit to explode.

"Exeter will decide if any further action needs to be taken. I've contacted the coastguard and the lifeboat people. Told them to look out for a bedraggled drowned butler! The lifeboat station have sent out a boat."

PC Hydon was bursting to speak out, but Sergeant Knowle jabbed him in the side.

"No, let him speak. Yes, Constable?"

"Sorry, sir, but there was no way we could have stopped 'im falling in the water. It was a complete accident on 'is behalf. 'E was a murderer, sir. Four women died at 'is 'ands. We did our best to apprehend 'im."

"I'm sure you did."

Inspector Wilkins looked at Alf with a smidgeon of compassion.

"What I need you to do now is go away and make out your report. Both of you. Make it as detailed as possible, especially the last two days. Send it to me as soon as possible. Tomorrow would be best."

"Yes, sir," said Elsie and Alf, almost in unison.

"That'll be all!"

Back at the Cobb Country House Hotel, Martha had phoned the hotel owner to let him know what had been happening in his own hotel in the past week. He swiftly appeared on the scene summoning an Assistant Manager from one of his other hotels to hold the fort whilst he considered what the future staffing of this hotel might be.

He stood behind the counter in reception studying the bookings for the next couple of weeks. "Are murders good for business?" he murmured. "Is any publicity good publicity?"

Martha and Emanuel stood beside him, not knowing whether to answer or just stay silent. The choice was made for them.

"The Assistant Manager will be here by the time you've served the evening meal, young lady. Emanuel, get back to your kitchen! Martha, you be his assistant."

Martha and Emanuel commenced the preparations for the evening meal.

Henry Soames, the Portobello Crooners' manager, arrived from London for a consultation with Cornelius and the band. They gathered in the lounge for Afternoon

Tea.

"Sorry, lads. Corny and I have decided, in the circumstances, to cancel the rest of the tour."

"Great!" said Albert. "What'll we do for wages?"

"Don't you worry. Once the national newspapers get hold of this story, we'll be booking you in for a brand new tour in bigger theatres. More money, bigger audiences, more opportunities. They'll all want to see Cornelius Spooner and his Portobello Crooners now. It could be the making of you!"

"Great!" repeated Albert.

"Wait a minute," said Johnny Toogood. "I may not want to carry on in the Crooners. It's quite nice around here. I may stay for a while."

Martha was standing by the tea trolley. She smiled.

Ella phoned the hospital for an update. She was put through to Imelda herself.

"They're releasing me soon. I was drugged but I'm going to be OK. Johnny Flynn, my boyfriend is an investment banker in the city. He's coming down to pick me up and take me back to London. He's booked a week in a convalescence facility somewhere in the Surrey hills. He's paying for everything!"

"That's great news. You look after yourself!"

"Thank you for everything. Please pass my thanks on to Frank. He saved my life. Thank you, thank you, thank you!!"

"Goodbye!" said Ella.

Ella then phoned Alice Aylesbeare. She was already on her way over from Budleigh Salterton to visit them. Half an hour later Annie Saxon sat in the lounge with Alice, Frank and Ella.

"This was an anniversary to remember!" said Ella.

"Don't worry. I'm sure next year will be less tumultuous," smiled Frank.

"One thing I noticed about Reeves was he was always tapping. Either his hands or his feet. Always tapping."

"That's because he was a drummer, wasn't he?" voiced Alice.

"A pretty good one by all accounts," commented Annie. "What a waste!"

"Do you know that lady policewoman from the front gates searched Reeves' room?" Ella added. "They found the other bag in his room."

"The contents were identical to the bag I had."

"I know," said Alice. "I did two copies just in case you didn't want to share."

Ella smiled. "We share almost everything!"

Frank asked Alice. "Did you know Annie was wife number six?"

"I did sort of guess. But you said you only wanted the facts, not conjecture. So that's what you got."

Frank chuckled and continued. "The policewoman also found copies of the invites to all five wives. Reeves sent the invites. *He* booked them rooms at the hotel, not Cornelius."

"Didn't you get one, Annie?"

"No. Perhaps he didn't know about me. I'm a late arrival. May well have saved my life!"

Ella changed the subject.

"As usual these dainty afternoon cakes are lovely!"

Everyone agreed and there followed a period of quiet enjoyment.

"Where's Cornelius?" asked Frank.

Annie smiled. "He's retired to his room for an afternoon

nap. These past few days really appeared to have affected him. He's looks worn out."

"What's the plan now the tour is off."

"I expect we'll go home and…"

The door opened and Cornelius Spooner, with a skip in his step, entered the lounge.

"Where's Henry? Henry Soames?" he boomed.

As if by magic, Henry appeared behind him at the lounge door followed by the band. Cornelius turned to greet them.

"Hello, Henry. I forgot, where's me money?"

"Already in the bank as usual!"

"Just checking." He wheeled towards the band. "Right lads, I'm off home. See yer when Henry's sorted us some new dates. Toodlepip!"

Cornelius Spooner pushed past Henry and the band and without even a glance at Annie, Alice, Frank or Ella, headed out of the room.

Annie sat there and tears began trickling down her face. "He never even said goodbye."

Alice patted her knee. "Annie, why don't you get your rucksack and stay with me for a few days? In fact, you can stay for as long as you like."

Annie nodded and smiled.

Ella turned to Frank. "You'll never guess what Imelda told me? Her boyfriend's name is Johnny Flynn. Coincidence or…?"

Frank held up his hand. "Don't even go there! It's time we were back in little old Otterbury. We've got our murderer. Or rather, the waves did!"

# POSTSCRIPT

To find out more about Frank and Ella and their East Devon Cosy Mysteries please visit the website: www.eastdevoncosymysteries.com

I can also be reached on:-

**Facebook**

www.facebook.com/pa.nash.182

**Twitter**

twitter.com/PANash49873070

**Pinterest**

www.pinterest.co.uk/EastDevonCosyMysteries/

or by

**Email**

info@eastdevoncosymysteries.com

Thanks for reading the fourth book in the East Devon Cosy Mysteries series.

*I would really appreciate a review (preferably positive!!) of this book. You can find me on Amazon at P.A. Nash's page.*

**The other books in the series**

The first book is called **Cidered in Sidmouth.**

The second book is called **The Dudleys of Budleigh.**

The third book is called **The Ottery Lottery.**

The next book (the fifth) in the series, when published, will be called **Brandied in Branscombe.**

The sixth book in the series, when published, will be called **Return to Sidmouth.**

# ACKNOWLEDGEMENTS

Many of the places mentioned in this book do exist. Some of the places exist only in the figment of my imagination. I'll leave it to you to come to East Devon to find out which are which.

# THE LYME REGIS & UPLYME
# CIRCULAR WALK

Frank and Ella's circular walk in Lyme Regis is based on one of Liz Jones series of commemorative walks. More information can be found the walk at lymeregis.org/walking.

Park in the Cobb Gate Short Term car park at the eastern end of Marine Parade. If full, try Bridge Street or Broad Street carparks.

*1. Cross over Broad Street between ironmonger and bookshop into Broad Street carpark and walk to the far end.*

From there take footpath to Town Mill and the Riverside Walk. After footbridge go straight ahead past Town Mill on your left before turning left by the Town Mill Cheesemonger into a narrow pathway leading to Riverside Walk.

At the end of Riverside Walk go straight ahead into Mill Green. When you see Dolphin Close on your left, look to your right and take the footpath along the left-hand bank of River Lim. Go over footbridge and turn left along road (named Jericho) before crossing over Woodmead Road into Windsor Terrace, still following the River Lim.

*2. At the crossroads with Roman Road and Colway Lane, go straight over onto a tarmac drive. Follow this drive and when it turns sharply right, take the footpath straight ahead. Follow the path over a footbridge and into a field (look out for a footpath marker), across field and through gate at end, across another footbridge. The River Lim is always in this vicinity in this part of the walk. Turn left passing an old mill on your right and onto then walk along an elevated wooded path above River Lim. At the end pass Honeysuckle Cottage and follow the track which leads into a road. This is Mill Lane. At the end of Mill Lane, pass between Brookside on the left and Waterside on the right before emerging at Spring Head Road.*

*3. Cross over Spring Head Road and enter The Glen (look for a footpath sign) and follow this wooded path to another road (Church Street) Look for another footpath sign and cross Church Street following the path (Aubrey's Way) to the main Uplyme to Lyme Regis road. Talbot Arms will be on your left.*

*4. Turn right and follow the main road, the B3165, for 50 yards until you reach Uplyme Village Hall on the left. Cross the road and pass in front of the village hall and through a gate (look again for a footpath sign) into the playing field. Keeping to the right-hand side of the playing field, cross the bridge and go through a gate ahead. There will be a sign -East Devon Way.*

Follow the path up and over the field and through the gate in the right-hand corner to a road. Turn left (look for another footpath sign) and go straight over Wadley Hill crossroads, soon veering right to join a country road entering from the left. This is Cannington Lane.

*5. Follow Cannington Lane past Holcombe Granary on the right, under the famous Cannington railway viaduct before turning left through a gate on your left just before a white house (look for a bridleway sign). Climb the field ahead towards a house. Go through the gate (look for bridleway markers) and along a path beside the house into the road ahead. Follow this road (Horseman's Hill) for about quarter of a mile.*

*6. Just past two cottages on the right you will see a footpath sign and steps leading into woods on the right. Go up the steps and follow the path steeply uphill over a stile.*

Follow the path along the left-hand hedge to a stile on your left. Cross this and the next stile and follow the path over a fourth and last stile on to a road, Gore Lane. Turn right to Ware Cross.

*7. Go straight over and follow the road, Ware lane, past Ware House Cottage and Ware House. When the road turns sharply left turn right onto a marked private drive (it is also a footpath).*

*8. Follow the track to a sign for a link to the South West Coast Path on left (Crow's Nest). Take this path and at a T-junction turn left (eastwards) along the coast path and through a gate. Look for the National Trust sign for Ware Cliffs.*

*9. Take path to the right and at cross paths take one to the right marked Lyme Regis The Cobb ½.*

Follow this path to a gate in the right-hand hedge (Not straight ahead) marked The Cobb ¼. Go through this gate and down the stepped path to the Monmouth Beach car park.

*10. Turn left past the Bowling Club and follow the road to the right of the Cobb Arms and along the sea front back to the Cobb Gate car park.*

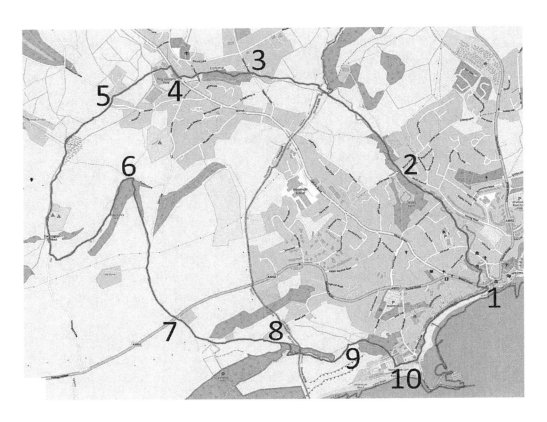

Mapping by OpenStreetMap

# ABOUT THE AUTHOR

PA Nash and his supportive wife moved to glorious East Devon nearly a decade ago having taken early retirement from his previous job in South East England. Not quite ready for a life of endless relaxation, PA has since dabbled as a website administrator for the South West Coast Path, an IT office assistant in a local school and a WordPress website designer. This is his first cosy mystery book.

I've read so many cosy mystery novels in the past ten years. Some series like MC Beaton's Hamish Macbeth and Agatha Raisin were excellent, others not so!

I thought I could put together a series based around an area of England. Everyone's written about the Cotswolds and the Midsomer counties, so I thought it would be best to avoid those areas. We live in a beautiful part of the South West of England. East Devon is full of quaint villages, relaxing towns, peaceful countryside and hidden gems. It's just waiting for a few juicy murders! The police presence is minimal. The population is not as full of old-aged pensioners as some would have you believe. Perhaps it's time to create a rival to Midsomer!

I enjoy walking so I've made use of the South West Coast Path and other footpaths in my books. Each book will have a selection of walks most reasonably fit people can complete. Some of the walks can be found on the excellent South West Coast Path Association's website.

I am in the process of creating a series of short cosy mysteries based around the towns and villages of East Devon.

\

Printed in Great Britain
by Amazon

87658767R00119